Secret Places

Vivian,
What a pleasure to get to
Know you. Be blessed!

Love
Starla Meister

Secret Places

STARLA MEISTER

TATE PUBLISHING
AND ENTERPRISES, LLC

Published by Tate Publishing & Enterprises, LLC
127 E. Trade Center Terrace | Mustang, Oklahoma 73064 USA
1.888.361.9473 | www.tatepublishing.com

Tate Publishing is committed to excellence in the publishing industry. The company reflects the philosophy established by the founders, based on Psalm 68:11,
"The Lord gave the word and great was the company of those who published it."

Book design copyright © 2014 by Tate Publishing, LLC. All rights reserved.
Cover design by Rodrigo Adolfo
Interior design by Mary Jean Archival

Published in the United States of America

ISBN: 978-1-63063-174-1
1. Fiction / Mystery & Detective / General
2. Fiction / General
14.01.02

Dedication

I dedicate this book to Yehovah. May he receive all glory and honor that is due him.

Acknowledgments

I give praise to Yehovah for he is worthy of all praise. It is he who gives me life, and to him be the glory.

I wish to thank my family and friends for their words of encouragement in the writing of this book. Mom, you were a big inspiration to me from a very young age and I believe that you passed on your God-given gift of writing to your children. I don't know how many times I persuaded one of my siblings into listening to the "next page" to make sure it "sounded all right." Big thanks go out to the GCHS staff members who inspired and challenged me and gave valuable editorial suggestions.

Thank you Ruth and Mom for all the work you put in on the scetches. Your time and efforts are appriciated.

To Ralf my dear husband: Thank you for the support that you have given me through this process. You are such an awesome man of Yahweh. I am blessed to be on this journey with you.

My
Secret Place

Friday, March 23

I remember the events of that Friday and being excited about the weekend. Differing weather patterns signaled the beginning of spring, yet there was heaviness in the air. Something was about to change, but then maybe it was just another storm brewing. This was sure to bring about the spring foliage which would blanket the earth with an array of color.

There was a clearing in the woods where our house sat, back in the hills of Kentucky. My twin brother, Jeff, and I stepped off the bus and headed toward the house. I heard the sound of the bus shifting gears as it went down the road kicking up a trail of dust. Next week was spring break and we wouldn't be missing the long dusty ride home on that rickety thing. I remember thinking, *Just eight more weeks until school's out*, and how that thought put a smile on my face.

But all thoughts of school were gone in an instant. Fear raced through my mind, instead, as our dog, Echo, ran straight for us, covered with blood and whimpering as if she had been beaten. Then we noticed the strange car sitting in the driveway. Uncertainty gave way to fear and then panic set in.

It was as if we read each other's mind when we both headed for our secret place in the woods behind our house. We raced past the large old barn and we ran as though we were running to escape all the possibilities of what could be wrong. It seemed an eternity, but we finally reached our destination.

Trembling with fear, we threw our backpacks on the floor of the cave, creating two clouds of dust as they hit the earth. Things seemed to move in slow motion and I could feel my heart pounding in my ears as the sweat and tears ran down my face. I turned to my brother for comfort; after all, he was the stronger one who was always seemingly able to handle the stressful situations throughout our young lives.

I noticed that Echo had followed and was now wagging her tail as if she was happy to have tagged along. She tried to lean against my legs, which was her usual custom when she wanted attention. I winced and moved away as my stomach churned at the sight of the still moist blood covering her small mixed breed body. We checked her from nose to tail but found no wounds. Where did all this blood come from?

—◦◦◦—

I remember when we first laid our eyes on Echo at the animal shelter. She was a bird dog mix that stood about a foot and a half tall, was snow white with cream-colored patches that were so light you didn't notice them from a distance, and had a long soft slender nose and amber-colored eyes. All of us agreed she was the one, so we adopted her and then dropped her off at the trainer. After picking her up from the trainer and having her in our home for several days, we grew fond of her and thought her to be a wonderful addition to the family.

My brother had been consoling me when he finally said, "Kylie, we need to decide what to do." I jumped at the sound of a shotgun blast in the distance. It sounded like it was coming from the direction of the house, but then hearing a gun being discharged in that area was quite a common thing, for people often hunted game around those parts. We knew we didn't have much time to make decisions, yet my mind drifted back to memories of the past.

It had been five years since we moved to Clear Creek, Kentucky from Palm Springs, California. Our dad, Sam, sat us down one day and, in his prosecuting attorney way, stated his case as to why we needed to get away from the "busy city life."

Our mom, Ann, joined Dad in telling us it would be a nice change. She told us, "The old rustic log cabin we are moving into is in need of some fixing, but it will be a good family project."

Our Mom was always fixing things up and so this old needy cabin was right down her alley. She was always on the move and seemed to have a lot of energy. Most everything she did revolved around us as a family. She cooked awesome meals and did a lot of canning. Mom also loved to rearrange the house about three or four times a year. She never dressed fancy and was so down to earth that she didn't even wear makeup. I couldn't imagine her any other way though because in my eyes she was perfect.

At first my brother and I sulked at the thought of leaving all our friends behind, as well as the things we were accustomed to in the city. We did though and for what? We left it all for this run-down log cabin in the middle of nowhere.

As it turned out, it didn't take long for our new place to grow on us once we had arrived and settled in. It became like an adventure—fixing up the cabin and becoming familiar with our new surroundings. We started doing things together as a family. Our parents took us on hikes, camping and fishing trips, church gatherings, and big barn dances. Barn dancing was something we had never been exposed to before, but as it turned out, it was quite fun.

Dad had always been a rather laid-back, gentle sort of person, which was part of what made him a good lawyer. Nothing seemed to get him too riled, so when he was upset, it was obvious to all who knew him. On the other hand, he would be so quiet sometimes that I would stare at him and wonder what he was thinking.

Dad told us he wanted us to learn to live on the land so he taught us all the things he had learned while being in Special Forces when he was younger. On some camping trips, all we took were our pocket knives and, wearing what we would normally wear on a Saturday, we would head into the woods for the entire weekend. We learned about different plant life, what we could and couldn't eat, how to start a fire without matches, how to hunt and fish for our meat, and how to build a shelter. He was an excellent teacher.

My brother and I started spending our free time roaming the woods that surrounded our house, and we eventually discovered what we both would call our secret place.

Our secret place was a cave located about a mile from our home. We found it after stumbling across some old pottery and utensils near the opening, which was covered over with a thicket of wild blackberries, so it was not easily noticed at first. We chopped some of the blackberries away, hoping to gain entrance, and once inside, we built a small fire on the floor of the cave which illuminated the big black hole. There was an immediate sense that someone had long ago made that place their home. We brushed aside all the cobwebs to find the old broken-down, makeshift bed next to one of the walls, which someone had taken the time to carve shelves into. On one of the shelves, we found an old dust-covered jug with a cork still in it. We found an old oil lamp with a book lying next to it, opened as if someone expected to pick up reading where they left off. Amid the debris were some old jars of canned goods. We decided they wouldn't be fit to eat, but we sat them on the shelves anyway with a sense of wanting to preserve the novelty and history of it all. We noticed an old, potbellied stove, and when we shined the light on the ceiling of the cave we could see where someone had built a chimney. What a treasure for two young city kids to stumble upon.

It became the highlight of our days to go to the cave and fix it up. We would climb to the top of the mound and clear the brush away from the chimney in hopes that we could use it someday. One day we found an old map and thought it to be interesting and a piece of art, so we hung it on the wall. We fixed the old bed to make it usable, and when there was time we made a new one resembling the old. We wanted desperately to be able to camp there some day, all by ourselves, if only we could get Mom and Dad to agree. Down the hill from the cave was a creek that we enjoyed playing in, especially on those hot summer days after our chores had been completed. That cave and its surroundings became our own little corner of the world where we dared to dream, work out our frustrations, plan our futures, or just play all day. We planted our flag and staked our claim on it, just as the settlers did in the Oklahoma land rush.

⚊⚊⚊

Now it seemed as if our parents and all we had come to know as home could be snatched from us.

Needing to find out what seemed to threaten our lives, we decided to make our way back to the house and check things out. Since there was no way of protecting ourselves, we had to be very careful not to be seen or heard. Being concerned that she would draw unwanted attention, we commanded Echo to stay at the cave.

Jeff stepped outside the cave while I stayed inside with Echo. Watching and listening, he walked fifty feet away from the entrance. When he felt there was no threat, we then headed toward the house. We followed the path for a ways and attempted to erase any noticeable tracks. For the remainder of the way to the house, we stayed away from the main trail and went through the woods on the leaf-covered earth, in case someone was following our tracks on that old, worn path.

We stayed away from all the other noticeable trails that the deer had worn through the woods as well. Some of these were obviously paths that animals had made; yet on our many adventures we found evidence leading us to believe that humans had cut some of these paths into the earth, like the time we found a bone-handled knife and an old, worn horseshoe lying next to one of the trails. On another one of our ventures, we had come across what looked to be the remainder of an old, one-room shack with the hitching post still standing and there was the evidence in our cave of the dust-covered belongings that had been left behind. How could one forget the old headstone that read LEVI WALLIS 1854-1906? Coming from the city, it was hard to imagine that people could actually live like that and I started thinking how they lived. A deep sadness came over me as I thought of their lives and how rough it must have been for them. I started to compare our lives to theirs and my thoughts wandered.

My mind kept drifting to the past and I had to keep reminding myself to stay focused on what was going on now, at that moment. It was important to stay alert, and be ready to make snap decisions and take quick action, should we need to.

Staying in the cover of the woods, we carefully circled the house, watching, waiting, and planning where we should spend the night. We noticed that the strange car was gone from the drive, but who it belonged to and where they were now was unknown. Time seemed to stand still. Looking at my watch I realized that three hours had passed since we had stepped off the bus. Suddenly I found myself wishing I were back in school, and once again I closed my eyes in an effort to stay focused.

There was still about thirty minutes of daylight left, so we made our way to the old barn and slowly opened the door. It made a squeaking sound that grated on my nerves like fingernails on a chalkboard. I thought it could surely be heard for miles as everything seemed to be exaggerated at this point.

My brother and I looked at one another then proceeded into the barn. Once inside, we went up into the loft where we both whispered a prayer asking God for guidance as well as protection of our parents and ourselves. While in the loft, we were able to look out the window that faced the house. There was a light on, but there was no sign of life. Although it was too dark to see much else, we felt it was safe enough to get a little rest before morning.

The night seemed to drag on forever, and though we were able to close our eyes, we couldn't turn our minds off. We were thankful when the morning sun peeked through the window to crowd out the darkness, which not only covered the earth but also our minds. With warmth from the sun came the hope of a new day and the possibility of an end to that nightmare.

Saturday, March 24

We carefully looked out the window with the desperate hope that the things of yesterday would somehow have been a bad dream. Instead there was a suffocating, solemn stillness filling the air, and the silence was so deafening that once again I could hear my heart pounding in my ears.

My mind wandered back to the last few weeks we lived in the city. There was a mix of emotions running through our family during that time. Leaving friends and relatives behind was the hardest thing for us to accept at the time.

I also remember there was something that seemed to be weighing heavy on our dad's mind, making him nervous and hard to get along with. Now, looking back on that day we left, it seemed as if Dad couldn't get out of the city fast enough. Something was definitely wrong as this was so out of character for our father. My brother and I couldn't put our finger on the source of the problem, but once we were far from the city, Dad's tensions seemed to fade and we forgot about it as well.

I could hardly believe that it had been five years since we packed our things and made the long journey to Kentucky.

—◁❧▷—

My brother must have been thinking about similar things. He spoke in a low, soft voice as he brought up the fact that Dad had been in the same anxious, edgy mood for the last week, just like before we left the city. He also reminded me how we were not allowed to give our friends from the city our forwarding address or new phone number. Dad told us that he would have the mail forwarded, and we didn't have a new phone number yet. Before leaving the city, Dad went through our things to make sure that we had nothing connecting us to our past lives. There was even the picture of the infant girl, who no one ever talked about, that had disappeared in the move to Kentucky. Jeff and I always thought her to be a distant relative or the like, and we were never lead to believe otherwise.

—◁❧▷—

After moving, our parents went as far as having our names changed, but once in a while, there would be a slip-up and our birth names, Michael and Moreh, would be used. At that time, we thought it a very peculiar thing to do to your own children.

When we moved, we were instructed to call Dad, Allen and mom, Ruth. Mom and Dad changed their last names from Longhenry to Carter, but for quite some time they had signed our last names as Deter, which is something we would find out about later. Come to think of it, we hadn't even had contact with our own relatives since leaving the city.

Our minds started spinning from all the odd memories that we had put away from five years ago. It was as if our pasts had been crowded out by our new surroundings and adventures, which, as children, was most important to us at the time. Now, we were waking up to the nightmare of what to do about our situation and how much of the turmoil was related to our father's bizarre behavior.

Something distracted my train of thought and brought me back to the present time immediately. With tensions as high as they were, anything as normal as the nocturnal animals scurrying about for food made our ears perk up. When we calmed our fears enough to peer over the loft to the barn floor, we caught a glimpse of Stinker, our name for the skunk who was known for stealing from Echo's food dish. We weren't too worried about Stinker, for the light of dawn would soon be encouraging him to find his way home where he would sleep the day away.

I know that Mom and Dad must have thought a lot about the things Jeff and I had given up in our previous lives: family, friends, and all the familiar things we had come to know as home in the city. Even though there seemed to be a lot more tense moments, until now, the city was familiar to us. When our location changed though, so did our lifestyle.

Mom and Dad started taking us to an old country church just down the road east of our house. We immediately felt at home and soon became members. This was one more thing that had changed since we moved here. It was a good change though, sort of like being part of a big family. It was as if they replaced the family we had left behind.

There was an older couple, Clara and Rich Vernon, whom we started to call Grams and Poppy, replacing the grandparents we left behind. They never had children of their own, though they cared for their neighbor's children when the mother was gravely ill. The mother pulled through, but her children spent most of that year with the Vernons, giving their mom time to fully recuperate.

Ed and his wife, Vivian, were our neighbors from whom we bought milk and eggs. They had eight children of which all were grown. Each one of them had moved away to the city where there was more opportunity. At church functions, Ed and Vivian would frequently talk of their children, which ones were married or soon to be and their many grandchildren or the one on the way.

Pastor Chuck and his wife, Adel, watched us on several occasions when our parents had to leave home "on business." They lived in a large, two-story log home which was almost like a lodge, but we always had fun at the Deter home when we stayed there. They were both well educated and always helped us with our homework, which was to be done right after we arrived home from school.

Jeff and I would gather eggs and help feed the critters. They had a couple of bottle-fed calves, pigs, several horses, and two milk cows. We were responsible for all but the milking. We didn't mind, though, as it was fun and we learned how to care for animals plus we learned how to ride the horses.

When chores were done, we sat down to a good home-cooked meal followed by homemade pie with ice cream. Then Pastor Chuck would play the fiddle while Adel played the piano and we all joined in the singing. Their home was noted for being alive with music, dance, and shared memories of when their children were growing up.

They rarely saw their children—Della, James, Darin and Erin—now that they all had moved so far away. But they kept in close contact and cherished every visit they had with them. Adel would always say, "Though they seem worlds apart on this earth, they are so very near us in our hearts."

Fridays—after homework, chores, and supper—we would all join in for game night. Having all this fun kept us from being so homesick for our parents, because when they were gone, it was as if they vanished. We never even got a phone call from them telling us that they missed us or how they were doing. They would just show up to pick us up on the day they said they would be home.

Mom and Dad started making these trips almost three years ago. They would leave for two weeks at a time and it was only every three to four months between the trips. In the last six months, they had been gone more frequently, and being gone more than they were at home was definitely a strain on us. There was never any talk of where they went or why. I guess we had just accepted this to be part of their job. When we did try to question them about where they were and what they did, the conversation was squelched.

Living in These Parts

Most of the country folks here believed in large families. People in these parts usually lived miles apart and thirty or more miles from a large town, so church functions were always well attended, as people cherished the fellowship of others.

We would enjoy potluck dinners that lasted for hours with games for the young and old alike. A game of baseball would take place in a field across the road and several horseshoe pegs would be set up closer to the picnic area. Younger children would play a game of chase while others would dare to touch the sky seeing how high they could swing. There were people who sat around catching up on current events while a lot of the older folks just enjoyed watching the scene unfold, cheering for their team.

There were a couple of old cowboys, Russell and Roy, who would sit around and reminisce about the times when they themselves were young. Being cousins and growing up together, they were often into mischief that one or the other of them had initiated. They told of breaking horses, cattle drives, near-death experiences, Old Settlers picnics, the best cow dogs they owned, losses in their lives, and finding their true loves. Each of their wives had gone on to be with the Lord, but as they would share stories of them, I couldn't help but notice the glistening tears that would roll down their cheeks. Their stories were so fascinating that I never grew tired of listening to them.

Jeff and I always found time to join in the games with the other children from church. These were pleasant times for my brother and me as we were able to relate to children our own age at these events. It was at these functions that we met our new friends Spencer and Sarah who were brother and sister. Although their parents didn't darken the church doors, they allowed Spencer and Sarah to come to some gatherings to socialize with other children. One time they introduced us to their friend Megan, who had come from out of state for a visit. Their parents were old friends and they had dropped Megan off while they went into Lexington for some sort of medical convention. I couldn't help but notice how pretty Megan was. She had a faint scar on her jaw line but that didn't take away from her beauty. She was a spunky outgoing girl who seemed to have everything going for her.

Several of the older folks commented on how much we looked alike saying, "If we didn't know any better we would swear you two were sisters."

Megan replied, "Well, you know the old saying. Everybody has a twin somewhere in the world."

I couldn't help but notice, as the wind swept her hair away from the side of her head and blew it wildly around, that her right ear looked like an earring had ripped through it. While we were playing, I asked her if she had ever had her ears pierced and she giggled as she said, "No, but everybody thinks that I had because of my birth mark."

She laughed as if she enjoyed telling me of her birth mark and I joined in the laughter. I got up the nerve to ask about the scar on her jaw and she got suddenly quiet, so I quickly changed the subject. We all spent the rest of the day laughing and losing ourselves in play.

Mrs. Deter would have Sarah and Spencer over to stay the night on several occasions while we were there. We always felt well cared for and thought of by the Deters. Going to church and having fellowship in this way had become a new way of life for us, a life we had grown to cherish very much.

We used to go to church occasionally when we lived in the city, but it was obvious that things had changed in our spiritual lives by moving here. We could tell that our parents had both grown closer to God. I remembered last Sunday at church when dad requested a special prayer for our family. He had always been so private about family matters that I wondered what could be wrong when he made this request. It made no sense at all, at the time, as things seemed fine then. Were they trying to shelter us from something, as many parents tended to do? Maybe they thought we were too young to comprehend, or maybe they just didn't want to alarm us. Back to the present, we were worried and were left with trying to bring all those pieces together to help us understand what was happening. Once again, we bowed our heads and sought God's guidance, believing he was the only one who could possibly help.

When we raised our heads and looked out the window, we noticed that Echo had made it back to the house. We both must have slept more soundly than we thought, because we also noticed a neighbor's vehicle sitting in the drive. We didn't know for sure how long he had been there and we were hoping that Echo wouldn't lead him to us, but it wasn't long before we saw Stephen step off the porch and head for his truck.

Stephen was the town sheriff who would stop by for a cup of coffee occasionally. It just so happened he wouldn't be getting his coffee this morning. As we both watched him drive off, I couldn't help but wonder if we missed our chance of getting the help we needed.

After an hour passed and we still didn't know what awaited us, we made our way to the house. Once inside, we searched the house and found a small pool of blood in the living room. It looked as if the house had been ransacked, but our parents were nowhere to be found. The tears began to flow once again, and this time my brother was as overwhelmed. What were we to do and where could we begin finding the answers to the mystery?

We decided to grab a few things from the house to take back to the cave for survival. We loaded our duffle bags and grabbed our survival kit, while making a mental list of other things that might be needed for the next few days. As we packed things, I thought to myself, "This wasn't our idea of someday being able to use the potbellied stove in that cave, but it looks as if this may be the case."

I noticed what looked to be a hurriedly scribbled note lying on the couch. It was in Mom's handwriting and all it said was, "Take my Bible." Could this be some clue that she was leaving for us?

We ran to her nightstand and opened the drawer where Mom kept her Bible. Upon hearing the sound of an approaching vehicle, I put her Bible in my duffle bag and we hurried out the back door. We started to run, with Echo on our heels, heading for the cave without looking back—that is, until we heard the vehicle drive past the house. We stopped at the edge of the woods to see if we could tell who it might have been. All we saw was the blue tailgate of a pickup with the big letters FORD on it. Believing it to be our neighbor Ed, we heaved a sigh of relief and continued on. We walked the rest of the way to the cave, skirting the path while carefully covering any noticeable tracks. We swept some old leaves across parts of the path and placed a few limbs on it as well, in hopes it would appear to be unused.

It took us longer than usual to reach the cave but once inside, we lit a few candles and pulled mom's Bible out. Holding it by the spine, Jeff shook it thinking some sort of evidence would appear. The only thing that fell to the ground was last week's church bulletin that Mom had written scripture on.

Looking at the scripture, we noticed it had nothing to do with Pastor Chuck's sermon from last week, so out of curiosity, we looked it up.

Turning to the scripture, John 8:32, our eyes carefully scanned the words: "Then you will know the truth, and the truth will set you free."

"The truth about what!" I shouted impatiently.

Jeff put his hand on my shoulder and pointed to the writing in the margin: "August 3rd 2002."

I turned to Jeff with tears in my eyes and whispered, "That's the day dad told us we were moving."

He nodded in agreement then he read the rest out loud.

> Jeff and Kylie, I fear the day will come when you will need to have some things explained to you. Your father and I have always tried to shelter you both, maybe a little too much. I only pray for your safety and that one day we will all be together again.

That was all she wrote along with another scripture, Psalm 61:1-4. But what did she mean by "we will all be together again"? She had written that nearly five years ago. How could she possibly know something was going to happen to them now? Turning the pages, we saw how Mom had underlined, in black ink, and highlighted, with yellow highlighter, a lot of scriptures in her Bible. Beside each one, a date and something she had written. It was like reading a diary in random order.

We read the next scripture:

> Hear my cry, O God; attend unto my prayer. From the end of the earth will I cry unto thee, when my heart is overwhelmed. Lead me to the rock that is higher then I. For thou hast been a shelter for me, and a strong tower from the enemy. I will abide in thy tabernacle for ever: I will trust in the covert of thy wings. Selah. Psalm 61:1-4

> August 4th 2002. It's two weeks until we move and I have the task of telling your grandparents that we will be moving to Alaska. Your dad and I had our mail forwarded to a false address there.

> We will have no further contact with other family
> members. Your dad and I feel the pain of this, but
> it is all for our safety. Psalm 62:1-2

We now realized that our parents had lied to everybody about where we had moved to. We being young had its advantages for them. All they told us at the time was that we were moving away from the city, figuring we would be too young to ask specifics. They were right.

Jeff read the next scripture aloud: "Truly my soul waiteth upon God: From him cometh my salvation. He only is my rock and my salvation; He is my defense; I shall not be greatly moved." Psalm 62:1-2

Next to it mom wrote:

> August 5th 2002. My children, I don't know if
> you will understand at such a young age what
> I am about to tell you. It has been two months
> since I asked Jesus to be Lord of my life. At the
> time I didn't realize we would be going through
> another trial, but I am so very thankful that
> whatever happens I can trust God to get us
> through. Romans 8:28

Looking back, I remembered a change in Mom even though I was only seven at the time. She used to cry a lot before she did that asking-Jesus-to-be-Lord-of-her-life thing. Even though it was hard to put the Bible down, our stomachs were telling us it was time to eat.

Yesterday's school lunch was the last time we had eaten. Mom usually put a snack in our backpacks for the bus ride home, but we had been too busy planning what we believed we would be doing for the weekend and spring break to bother eating them. With all that had gone on after getting off that bus, we just hadn't thought of eating, but now our bodies were telling us it was time for some nourishment. We didn't have much of an appetite, so we nibbled on the snacks silently, thinking of our parents and wondering where they could be and if they were still alive.

After finishing our snacks, we unpacked our duffle bags, storing supplies on the shelves and throwing the sleeping bags on the beds. We made our way to the creek to wash Echo off so she could dry before the night came and chilled her. As darkness fell in the woods, that night we turned to God in prayer, asking for comfort and guidance.

After saying amen, Jeff said with a blank stare, "Tomorrow is Sunday. What do you think we should do?"

Knowing how friendly the neighbors were, we agreed that we should go to church to keep them from stopping by later.

"Goodnight, Sis." I heard Jeff whisper.

"Night," was all I could say back.

After a long silence and a lot of thought, exhaustion finally took my body in sleep.

Sunday, March 25

Morning came once again and we had to prepare for the day. We made our way back to the house. Upon careful approach, things appeared fine, but we were still cautious, looking in every direction for any sign of danger. We put Echo in her pen, fed, and watered her then went inside to get ready for church. Jeff kept watch while I took a quick shower and slipped into my clean clothes then it was my turn to stand guard while he got ready. Before we left, we put things back the way they were and made sure that our dirty clothes were put in the hamper. We locked the front door and went out the back. With mom's Bible clutched in my hand, we got our bikes from the barn and rode them to church, just like we had done many times before.

Mrs. Deter greeted us at the door of the church then asked, "Where are your folks today?"

Pastor Chuck shot a questioning glance in our direction then turned to his wife and said, "They're probably away on business Adel. Don't you remember Allen stopping by and telling us they thought that Kylie and Jeff would be fine on their own the next time they had to leave town?"

"Yes, but I thought that he said they would let us know when they were leaving so that we could stop to check on them and stay with us if they so chose."

"Well, as busy as things can sometimes get, maybe they each thought the other had called."

We were hoping they wouldn't start asking questions, for we didn't know what was going on, and at this point, we didn't know who to trust with our secret.

That conversation ended as Adel quickly invited us for dinner and we politely accepted. We knew they wouldn't take no for an answer plus we both needed the good hot meal along with the security of being in a safe place. They lived next door to the church, which was a convenient arrangement for them, so after the final amen was said and people were finished visiting, we all headed to the pastor's house.

We sat down for a Sunday dinner of fried chicken, corn on the cob, and mashed potatoes with gravy. For dessert there was fresh apple pie with a scoop of homemade ice cream. This was the regular menu for most church folks' Sunday dinner around these parts.

After the food was blessed, we all dug in, and for a moment, it felt as if things were normal, causing us to let our guard down for a moment. We must have been eating like half-starved children, for when I looked up, Pastor Chuck and his wife were staring at us with a bewildered look on their faces.

Pastor said, "Are you children getting enough to eat while your parents are gone?"

Wanting to avoid any further questioning, I quickly said, "Yes, and I'm sorry Mrs. Deter, this chicken is just so good we forgot our manners. I know M-mom would scold us if she knew we were behaving this way. Please forgive us."

I had hoped she didn't notice my hesitation when I spoke of Mom. It was hard pretending things were normal when our world was upside down.

She told us that things were just fine and that we shouldn't worry; nothing would go beyond these walls, and with that, dinner continued without further questioning.

After the meal, we helped with the cleanup then we thanked our hosts and prepared to leave. Mrs. Deter was kind enough to have packed some leftovers for supper then we hopped on our bikes and hurried down the road toward home. Once the bikes were put away, we let Echo out of her pen and headed for our secret place.

After opening mom's Bible, we went back to the last scripture that had been posted:

> And we know that all things work together for good to them that love God, to them who are the called according to His purpose. Romans 8:28

> August 6th 2002. When things seem to be going all wrong, I want you to remember this verse and believe in it. It has helped me to keep going forward. Love, Mom. Romans 3:23

Mom had stopped leaving messages next to scriptures from the time we moved until about a year ago. Something must have changed; it was like she felt safe and relaxed right after moving, but something stirred her to write more before they came up missing. She hadn't stopped reading her Bible though; there was evidence of that as she continued to put dates and forwarding scriptures next to each passage that she had read. We continued to read the scriptures that she had forwarded.

Mom had a heavy load on her shoulders, but she had the joy of the Lord in her heart. This was known to us in the way she sang praises and whispered prayers often, as she worked around the house and throughout the days. Even though we were younger, we could sense this dark cloud hanging around now and again but Mom chose to live her life for Christ. Not once did she put herself before God or taking care of us. She always chose to take the path that led to the firm foundation that kept her steady.

On the blank parts of the pages, she would have words of encouragement and statements of how she was growing in her faith. There were scriptures that told us that we were all born with sin in our lives, how Jesus died to pay for our sin, and if we ask for forgiveness, He would be faithful and just forgive us. Looking back we could see the definite change in the way our parents lived their lives compared to before. Whatever our parents were going through, Mom left no doubt in our minds that God would carry them to the other side of it safely.

If God was taking care of our parents, what did he do with them and why did he leave us alone?

We started a small fire in the stove to take the evening chill off before eating our leftovers. As darkness covered the land, confusion filled our minds and we prayed, asking God to help us understand and believe the way our parents did and to keep us safe and direct us in what to do next.

Someone to Trust

Monday, March 26

We hadn't planned on spending our spring break trying to solve a mystery, but as the morning sun made its way to the forest floor, we were getting ready for another day of investigating the disappearance of our parents.

We woke to the sounds of critters rustling the leaves that carpeted the forest floor. A brave squirrel strutted right up to a lone chip that was lying on the floor of the cave, grabbed it, and ran before Echo could challenge him for it. Jeff and I both laughed as Echo stood there with her head cocked to the side and an expression of disbelief in her eyes. This laughter was a welcome relief from the undeniable tensions of the previous days.

"Well, I guess it's time for our breakfast now," Jeff said with a grin.

After giving thanks, we ate the homemade granola which we had grabbed from the house. Mom always took the time to make what she referred to as "the healthy stuff." We were thankful for all that she had done for us, and we missed her dearly.

After breakfast, Jeff read more from the Bible, and then we decided to go back to the house to straighten it up just in case someone from the church stopped to check on us. We didn't want to let on that anything was wrong.

While cleaning, we searched for further clues as to what had happened and that was when we noticed the bloody footprint with drops of blood trailing to Dad's study. The print was too large to have been Mom's or Dad's, but that didn't mean the blood wasn't theirs. Did we miss seeing this due to the chaotic rush when we were here Saturday? Or had someone been back and made this track? Whose blood was this, and was it from the same source as the blood we had washed off of Echo? Sunday was filled with getting ready for church, the lunch afterwards, and such that we hadn't taken the time to check for more clues.

Walking into Dad's study was like seeing the aftermath of a tornado. Whoever had been here was determined to find something that must have been very important to them. We noticed another note that was pegged to dad's bulletin board behind the desk where we often found Dad doing bookwork, reading the paper, or studying his Bible. Again, it was in Mom's handwriting. When I finished reading the note, I snatched it from the board and put it in my pocket.

It took us until 1:00 pm to get the house cleaned up and looking like someone actually lived there. After straightening things and finding no further clues, we left the house and headed for our new home.

When we got back to the cave, I pulled the note out of my pocket. It had yet another Bible reference on it. I handed the Bible to Jeff and gave him the scripture to look up.

Mom had started writing notes by the scriptures again and they told of how much she and Dad loved us, were praying for us, and longed for us to someday understand the love of Christ.

Jeff turned the pages until he reached the scripture that was on the note, Psalm 91:1-6, then he read:

> He that dwelleth in the secret place of the Most High shall abide under the shadow of the Almighty. I will say to the Lord, He is my refuge and my fortress: my God; in him will I trust. Surely he shall deliver thee from the snare of the fowler, and from the noisome pestilence. He shall cover thee with his feathers, and under his wings shall thou trust: his truth shall be thy shield and buckler. Thou shalt not be afraid for the terror by night; nor for the arrow that flieth by day; Nor for the pestilence that walketh in darkness; nor for the destruction that wasteth at noonday. KJV

Mom wrote:

> March 2nd 2006. "I have followed you to the cave three times in the past month. It was hard to spot, when I tried to find it on my own. I thought I had better find out where this "secret place" is that you both refer to when you ask to play in the woods.
>
> Your dad and I have visited the cave on several occasions, while you were in school. We both believe it to be a safe place for you.
>
> I see why you enjoy your secret place, and this is why I am writing a note to you, along with this scripture. You see, I believe that everyone should have a secret place, where they can go to get away from everything and just be alone to think. My

most favorite place is the loft of the old barn. I go there early in the mornings to be alone with God. It's easier to communicate with Him when I am away from all the distractions of life.

My prayer for you is that you will have a personal relationship with Him, as I do, to know how much He really loves you and desires to be your God. This scripture also tells how He will take care of His followers, no matter what is going on around us or what time of the day it is.

My hope is that you find your true secret place in Him.

Love Mom. Romans 3:10

Some of the things that mom had written started to make sense as we read them. Thinking of all the changes that she and dad had made in their lives, including their behavior and habits, began to make us aware of what they had found in their relationship with God. We had even come across a poem that mom had written in the margin of her Bible. As Jeff read it, the flood gates opened causing water to flow down our cheeks.

Storms

The storms had me surrounded
I could find no way out
They all said, "I'll be your friend."
But I had a lot of doubt

The clouds finally broke away
And silence hushed the wind
Morning will be a new day
And I'll find the rainbow's end

There's not a pot of gold
As many people say
But hope is mine to hold
To make it through another day

Healing is a journey
That we all take now and then
But that journey is made easier
With all the people whom we call friend.

During the storms of our lives, God has definitely sent many of his children to us who have become our friends and have helped us through all our heartaches. I've learned to trust in God and count on these people, whom he has blessed us with, as dear friends.

Love,
Mom

We were concerned about what it was that Mom and Dad had endured that was so extremely difficult. There was a curiosity about the faith in God that Mom talked so much about. "It must have been their faith in God that helped them through their troubles." I said softly.

This sparked an interest in wanting to know more about what they had, so we talked about the possibility of setting down with Pastor Chuck to discuss this stirring in our hearts. Then, realizing that the pastor was more than likely not aware of our parents' strange disappearance, we reconsidered talking to him at that point. This led us to wonder if there was anybody in the church whom we could talk to about our dilemma. Time seemed to pass by so fast while we were reading and discussing all that we had read that we lost track of what time it was getting to be.

It was late afternoon and our stomachs were letting us know that we hadn't eaten in a while, so we pulled some food from our duffle bags and prepared to eat. After giving thanks, we sat in silence and ate the leftovers that we had taken from the house.

Both of us had become overwhelmed with our situation and had started feeling all alone in the world, but we were determined not to give up.

We planned to take what was left of that day and decided who we might trust to tell about all that had gone on the last three days. We had come to the point wherein we no longer wanted to be alone in our troubles.

Before evening, we went on to read the next scriptures that mom had noted:

> As it is written, there is none righteous, no, not one. Romans 3:10

> For all have sinned, and come short of the glory of God. Romans 3:23

> For the wages of sin is death; but the gift of God is eternal life through Jesus Christ our Lord. Romans 6:23

> But God commendeth His love toward us, in that, while we were yet sinners, Christ died for us." Romans 5:8

> If thou shalt confess with thy mouth the Lord Jesus, and shalt believe in thine heart that God hath raised Him from the dead, thou shalt be saved. Romans 10:9

Mom wrote beside the last scripture:

> March 3rd, 2007. My dearly loved children, I used to think that if I was good enough in this life I would be allowed into heaven. This scripture tells me that no one is good enough to get there on their own, because we have all sinned. It also tells us that the wages, or cost, of sin is death. The pastor at our old church in the city had me read these scriptures, and he explained them to me. This is when my eyes were opened to the truth that God does love us. He loves us enough that he sent his own Son to die to pay for our sins. We must believe this and ask him to forgive us. When we do this with a sincere heart, he will be our God and we will be his children. The Bible is so full of his love and direction for our lives. He is our provider and will see us through the things we sometimes don't understand. We need only to trust him. Sometimes, God will send people into our lives who can help us understand his ways. Pastor Chuck and Adel are two of God's trusted servants. Your dad and I want you to know that if you need someone to talk to you can trust them to tell the truth about things.
>
> Love Mom

After reading everything that Mom had written, we decided that we would pay Pastor Chuck a visit tomorrow to let him know what was going on and inquire about the stirring, almost-empty feeling inside. We were ready to seek help in finding out about our parents, as well as learn more about the scriptures.

We spent a long night tossing and turning, thinking and discussing how to approach the pastor about our predicament. After all, how does a child begin to tell anyone of the horror of the past three days, what with the uncertainty of where our parents could be and if they were still alive. We could only hope, pray, and trust God to take care of us and them.

Tuesday, March 27

Morning came with much anticipation of how the talk with the pastor would go. To prepare ourselves, we prayed then read the Bible. Following the trail of scriptures that Mom had written had been difficult for us. We always read with a hope that Mom would leave us some sort of clue about what had caused them to go missing. She did, however, stir our spirits in wanting to know more about having a personal relationship with Jesus. That morning, while flipping the pages to the passage, Jeff stopped suddenly as he noticed that the note beside the scripture was in Dad's handwriting. Jeff took a deep breath of air then started to read, skipping the Bible verses, as the note had captured his eye.

> Jeff and Kylie, we love you both so much. Your mom has told me about writing all the messages during her Bible reading.
>
> When things started happening these last three months, we sat down, wrote you a letter explaining what you should do if we had to leave unexpectedly, and we had a talk with the pastor about this as well. It is important for you to know that you can trust Pastor Chuck. We left the

letter in his care after telling him what we could about our situation.

All the things I have taught you about how to survive in the woods was intended for you to be able to make it on your own should the need arise. Your mom and I pray for your safety. We want you to know that we do everything we can to create a safe environment for you.

I know that people are praying for us and that somehow God will work things out.

Love, Dad

After reading this, we were assured that going to the pastor with our troubles was the best thing to do and that one of our prayers had been answered. We finally believed we could trust someone and was assured of who this person was. Could it be that God put Pastor Chuck in our lives for such a time as this?

We were almost to the house when we heard someone calling our names. We noticed the pastor's old pickup parked in the driveway then heard the shrill sound of the barn door opening as he and his wife exited the building. Echo started barking and ran ahead as if she was happy to be the first to greet them. They spotted us then stood waiting at the doorway of the barn.

Jeff and I must have had a look on our faces that told them that something was awry. Pastor Chuck turned to his wife and nodded as if they had had something between the two of them confirmed.

Mr. and Mrs. Deter opened their arms as if to say, "Come, rest now, it will be alright." As I reached Adel, I laid my head on her chest and tears started to flow as if the flood gates had been opened from deep within. They each held us for a moment then suggested going to their home. We put Echo in the back of their old pickup then we hopped in the front seat with them.

It seemed to take forever as we rode in silence to the church parsonage. It felt as if we were going to a funeral, with no words spoken, only a sniffle or someone clearing their throat to choke back the tears. Once inside we were asked if we needed anything to eat or drink. We both accepted a drink of ice-cold lemonade. While Adel went to get the drinks, Pastor Chuck excused himself and went to his study.

Returning with a large manila envelope in one hand and his Bible in the other, the pastor took a seat between us on the couch and slowly opened the envelope. Adel had already brought our drinks and was sitting next to me.

Before reading the letter, Pastor Chuck bowed his head and spoke a brief prayer, asking God for guidance and peace. This was a very emotional moment for all of us. As I raised my head after "Amen," I noticed both Pastor Chuck and his wife had tears streaming down their faces.

While unfolding the letter, Pastor Chuck told us of the day that Dad came to him and confided in him only some of the troubles that had risen. He said that Dad and Mom wanted Jeff and me to be taken care of and to know that we would be kept from harm. They had also told Pastor Chuck and Adel that there would be an occasion when they would need to leave with little time to plan, but that they would only be gone for three days and that Jeff and I would be allowed to stay on our own for that period of time.

The pastor and his wife had a very solemn look about them as he told us how much he and his wife loved our family and would do their best to protect us. Then he took a deep breath, raised the letter, and began to read.

Jeff and Kylie,

Your mother and I are involved in something that can't, for your safety and the safety of others, be discussed at this time. For this reason we have set some things up, in order for you to be taken care of in our absence. We made arrangements for Pastor Chuck and his wife to be your legal guardians. This is why we had changed your last names long ago. The house and property is in their name as well. We set it up to look like we rented the house from them and that you were their grandchildren who were living with them.

We met the pastor and his wife long before we moved to Kentucky and they have been a vital part of our lives, helping us through many problems. They agreed to help us and told your mom and me that they were led by God to do so. They will tell you how God led them to help us, but for now just know that you are safe in their keeping.

We both know how confusing things must be for the two of you, and for this we are heartbroken and sorry. No child should have to go through such fear and uncertainty as you have in your lives.

We love you very much and will be praying for you every day.

Love,
Mom and Dad

Somehow my brother and I knew that this letter would not give us straight answers as we hoped it would. What is it about adults that make them think withholding information from their children is the best thing to do? Don't they know that for us, it only adds fuel to our desire to find out all that is going on?

Pastor Chuck had realized that there was something else in the large envelope and checked its contents again. When he tipped the envelope, something fell out and we all looked to see it was a key to something, but we hadn't a clue what it was for.

Jeff and I thought it looked to be a spare house key and didn't think anything more of it.

After the evening meal was finished and everything was cleaned, we all gathered in the living room where Adel started playing the piano. Pastor Chuck picked up the violin and joined in playing gospel music. We sang and danced for quite some time. This always seemed to cause an unexplainable drawing to God. It was as if I could feel him smiling and enjoying our songs for him. After the songs, Pastor Chuck read a passage from the Bible. It was some of the same ones Mom had talked about and highlighted in her Bible. They were what I would later know as the Roman's Road to Salvation. That night the Pastor led both Jeff and me in a prayer, and we told God we were sorry for our sins and asked him to forgive us. I immediately felt a change. It was as if I had been in a fog and the sun burned it all away so that I could see and understand things like never before. I was so full of this joy that I couldn't describe. Pastor and Adel told me it was the "joy of the Lord." I could sense the change in Jeff as well. Before we went to bed, we talked about how we could use the rest of spring break to further investigate this mystery. This night it seemed so much easier to fall asleep.

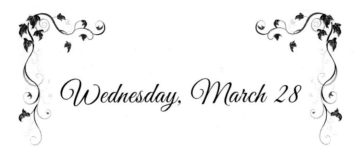

Wednesday, March 28

Morning broke with the anticipation of where to start picking up clues to this puzzle. We bowed our heads in prayer, thanking God for the security of a home with adults to watch out for us and also help us carry our heavy burden. We also asked God to send angels to watch over our parents and bring them home safely to us and to help us find the answers we so desperately needed.

Pastor and Adel must have thought that we needed the rest, as they didn't disturb us until almost 10 a.m. Little did they know that neither of us could sleep and that we had been up since three that morning trying to figure out what we could do.

As we brainstormed, we came up with the idea of making a time line. It was like putting together the outside edges of a puzzle and making the rest easier to fill in. Our problem seemed to be finding all the edges.

We decided to go way back to when we lived in the city, even to the first memories of our childhood, and work our way to today. Mom's Bible came in handy, as we believed it was a major clue in our line of events. When reading her Bible, we sensed that she desperately wanted to tell all that she knew but held back knowing the severity of the situation. We still believed that we could gather clues from these notes that she left.

Pulling out paper and pencil, we each started jotting things down as we remembered them. Once each of us was done with our lists, we compared notes and put together parts of our timeline. Knowing it would take longer to read the rest of what Mom had written, we added the little bits that we had already read.

Seeing the time line also sparked remembrances of other events, such as when we first started school here. It seemed as if the pastor and his wife had known our parents long before we even moved here and that was after all explained in the letter that Mom and Dad had left with Pastor Chuck. They, not our parents, were the ones who got us enrolled and took us to our first day of school. Anytime we needed to be picked up, guess who came to get us? The only time we actually were taken anywhere by our own parents was when we attended church services. At first our parents always had an explanation as to why they couldn't take us places with them. After a while, the excuses stopped, as we soon accepted it to be normal.

There were many times during the last year and a half of living in the city that Mom had hurried us out the back door of our house, across the fence, and into the house next door. She would always tell us that it was time to check on Dorothy, the elderly neighbor who was supposedly very ill.

We would feed her cat, water her plants, and take care of her fish while Mom checked in on her. Mom never let us visit with Dorothy though, saying she was too sick to visit with children, so we never even knew what she looked like. During this time, we started noticing the emotional change in Mom. She used to cry a lot when all that first started. About three months into this constant pressure of checking on Dorothy, Mom seemed more at peace. The question remained as to what had taken place in Mom's life that caused the dramatic emotional changes.

We visited Dorothy more frequently as the days went by. In fact we started spending several nights a week at her home. She must have been very sick indeed as Mom would always stay in Dorothy's room when we were there for the night.

After dwelling on these things, we both came to the conclusion that it was time that we investigated further for more answers. But we would have to pick things up again the next day, for we needed to help out with the chores, and the Deters had other plans for the remainder of the day.

After lunch and chores were finished, we asked to be taken to our house so that we could check on things. Going through the house, it seemed that nothing more had been disturbed, but Jeff had the great idea of checking the answering machine for new or old messages.

I hollered for Pastor Chuck, and we checked the messages. There was one message and it was a voice we didn't recognize.

"Hello, is anybody home? Come on, if anybody's there, pick up. Please answer your phone. We stumbled on some information and you could be in danger."

We heard another voice in the background yelling, "Hang up. We need to get out of here. It's not safe!"

There was a loud click then silence. The caller ID displayed a disappointing "Unknown" on the screen. We didn't think to check this on Monday when we came to clean the house. The time and date on the phone read March 23rd, 11:37 am. That would have been Friday. The day our nightmare began.

Jeff and I weren't about to give up hope now. Someone out there knew something about our parents and what was going on. So, as discouraging as the call sounded, we both thought of it as hope in finding our parents.

After seeing our response to the message on the answering machine, Pastor Chuck and his wife had realized that we, as children, were beyond our years in maturity and they treated us as such. At the same time, they also realized we were still children and therefore encouraged us to have as much of a childhood as humanly possible, in light of all that we have been through and continued to experience.

We all took a walk to the cave, where Jeff and I introduced our humble dwelling to Pastor Chuck and his wife. It was the highlight of the day to show them around and to know they were in agreement that our secret place was not only peaceful but also a very safe place, as it was tucked away behind the foliage that covered the entrance. They encouraged us to come here should we feel threatened in any way, telling us if anything should happen they would know where to look first. Later we took supplies to the cave, like some of Adel's canned food, things that would keep for a long time to come, and large waterproof and critter-proof containers with blankets, kerosene, lighters, and cooking and eating utensils. Mom and Dad had told the pastor and his wife about the cave but had never shown it to them, so it was all very interesting for them.

Before returning to the Deter home, we packed extra clothes and a few items we might need while staying with them. We packed light though, still not wanting to think of the possibility that we might not be returning home. The Deters didn't pressure us in any way and allowed us to take only the few things we decided on.

As evening fell on this place we now called home, we both pondered the events of the day. As my brother and I turned in for the night, we each said "good night," knowing it had a deeper, more hopeful meaning than before.

I sunk into bed, my body heavy with exhaustion, yet I managed to hear the voices from down the hall. Voices so familiar I sat straight up in bed straining to hear more. Was I just so tired and longing for mom and dad, or was it really their voices I was hearing? I nearly burst into tears at the thought of seeing them again, but I held those tears deep inside as long as I could.

When I was younger, I used to have the most vivid nightmares, usually waking the whole family up with bloodcurdling screams of terror. I eventually outgrew them, but my brother, being my twin, was still sensitive to this, so when he heard me sobbing he entered my room. "Sis," he said, in a soft, calming voice, "you were having a bad dream."

I had actually been asleep for a couple of hours and was dreaming that I heard Mom and Dad. I started bawling uncontrollably, brokenhearted at the thought of even hearing our parents' voices again. It must have been listening to the answering machine today that triggered the dream.

It took me nearly an hour before I was calm enough to sleep again. Having my brother sleeping on the floor in my room gave me the comfort I needed to finally drift off to sleep.

Thursday, March 29

I must have been more exhausted than I realized, for I didn't wake up until midmorning to the creaking sound of the door opening. It was my brother coming in to check on me and to open the curtains to allow the sun to lighten the room.

I felt the warmth of the sun as the rays came through the window and touched my face. This caused floods of fond memories to go rushing through my mind. Mom used to come in our rooms in the mornings and pull the curtains back, telling us it was too beautiful a day to sleep in, then she would gently remind us of our chores which needed to be done before school.

The sound of Jeff's voice brought me back to the present.

"Sis," he whispered.

"Yes," I answered.

"Just checkin' to see how you're doin'."

"I'm good. What time is it anyway?"

"It's almost ten thirty. I'll let you sleep some more if you want."

"No, I'll be out as soon as I get dressed," I answered as he was closing the door.

When I reached the bottom of the stairs, I was greeted by Mrs. Deter. She asked how I was doing and if I would like some breakfast. Jeff had chosen to wait to eat breakfast with me, but the Deters chose to eat at their normal time. They did sit with us at the table, drinking their morning coffee as we ate. Each of us must have been in deep thought as there were very few words spoken during our meal.

When breakfast was finished and chores were done, Jeff and I worked on our time line. We replayed the phone message over and over in our minds. Neither of us had recognized the voices on the message, but we hoped that they would call again soon. In the meantime, we would keep ourselves busy working on what we already had, until later in the day when we decided to go to the house and check on things.

As we all climbed into the pickup, we noticed a strange vehicle drive by with out of state tags. People in those parts usually took note of unfamiliar vehicles as they were not something one saw too often there. If someone was expecting company from out of the territory, it was spread throughout like wild fire so everyone would keep an eye out for the unknown vehicle. It was just one of the ways we watched out for each other there; it was sort of like our version of the neighborhood watch program. No one had told of visitors coming for several weeks, so we had to assume these were strangers—in search of what, we didn't know.

We drove on down the road toward the house and the strange vehicle was parked in our driveway. The pastor drove right on by, but we all watched to see two people on the porch. It appeared that one was knocking on the door while the other was peering through the window. It seemed to be more dangerous to be stopping at the house, but we desperately needed to be able to search the house for more clues or possible messages on the answering machine. What if Mom and Dad were trying to contact us?

Pastor Chuck decided to drive on in to town and do some errands while trying to find out if anybody had news on the strangers. He also planned to stop at the homes of some of his parishioners to glean any information they may have concerning our out of state guests.

The church we had attended since moving here had proved to be a tight-knit group of people who looked out for each other. It was like one large family. What was one's business was all's business, which could help in times like these. We accepted each other warts and all, and the beauty of it all was the trust in one another. People honored others and wouldn't dare to cross another and cause mistrust. Pastor Chuck told us that there had been feuds in those parts long ago until everyone came together to search for some children who got lost in a blizzard on their way home from school. He shared with us that sometimes it takes disaster or tragedy to bring people together.

We stopped at Dukes Grocery to pick up some food supplies then went on to the town's hardware store. We had one last stop to make, Smiley's Quick Stop and Tire Shop with a movie rental inside.

Mr. Logan owned the place and had always offered soda to all his patrons' children. When we tried to pay, he'd always tell us, in his strong Kentucky accent, "T's o me. Youins jus enjo et." He was always such a happy person, but he had visible scars that made us wonder what had happened. Children can be innocently curious at times, and so we were, and we asked the question that adults would be too embarrassed to ask. "What happened?"

Mr. Logan told us, "'Tis been so long 'go. All I 'member's thankin' the good Lor' ahm still her'."

You could tell that he had grown up in these hills just by the way he talked. You could also tell that he had the love of Jesus in him as he was always smiling, helping others, and singing of his love. I'm sure his continual smile is how he got his nickname Smiley, which in turn became the store's name.

While we were fueling up the truck, that same strange car pulled in right next to us on the opposite side of the pump. We all held our composure as the pastor went inside to pay for the fuel and have a word with Smiley. As they spoke, they had their backs to us, and it seemed they were talking about tires as the pastor pointed to different ones that hung on the wall. Adel asked us if we wanted to check out a movie, so we all went inside to browse. On the way into the store, we talked about which movie we would be looking for. One of the strangers nodded and smiled. I just smiled back as we continued to walk, but all the while my stomach was churning inside.

We all were quite friendly with these strangers on the outside, but deep within there were rivers of suspicion flowing through our veins. At this point, there were few people to trust and no chances to be taken. Before leaving, we absorbed as much information as possible about these strangers for later use. We studied their faces which were kind but very serious-looking and business-like. They were dressed in semicasual clothes and drove a dark Lincoln Continental with darkened windows and Virginia license plates.

Jeff took a deep breath, exhaling slowly and whispered, "Do you remember what kind of car was on our driveway when we got off the bus Friday evening?"

"No, I was so scared that all I could think of was running. Do you remember what it looked like?"

"Well, I remembered that it was a large car with dark windows, but I don't know for sure what kind it was or what tags it had on it."

Jeff and I had both climbed into the pickup and the pastor was closing the door when one of these men spoke to him. He flashed us a quick wink before turning to speak to the man. With the window up, we could barely make out what was being said, but to roll the window down could have been taken as suspicion on our part, so we waited. Pastor Chuck accepted what looked to be a business card from the man and shook his hand. The pickup door opened, the pastor slid behind the wheel, and we all heaved a huge sigh of relief.

As we pulled out into the road, the questions began to flow. Adel even joined in with her own, asking, "Chuck, who were those men and what was on the card they gave you?"

Then we joined the interrogation.

"Do you think they know who we are?"

"What if they know about us and our parents?"

"Do they know where our parents are and if they are alive?"

Then Jeff asked, "Are we safe here anymore and will we have to move away?"

With all our intense questioning, Pastor Chuck couldn't get a word in edgewise, so he waited patiently for us to calm down and he began to answer our questions. He answered according to what he found out at the fuel station and he never once put on pretences of knowing more. He was very open with what he knew. After what we had already been through, he figured we could handle what he told us.

"Well, they said their names are Fred and Bill and they said they are here to find you and keep you two safe. Sort of like body guards, I reckon. I don't know if they can be trusted but they gave me a card and asked me to call if I had any information that I thought might be helpful. They say they don't have much to go as far as a description of you two, but they do have something to say when they find you, then you will know that they are who they claim to be. They say that they have been sent by your parents."

With those words, Jeff and I sat up in our seats with a fresh hope in our hearts and tears streaming down our cheeks. When Pastor Chuck noticed our joy, he hesitated then spoke in a soft, calming voice.

"You do realize that we need to be very careful here and check things out before we even think about calling these men? This is all for your safety. People like this will and can be baiting us and trying to harm you."

Pastor saw the look on our faces and reminded us not to give up hope and that it may turn out to be a very good thing, but we needed to have patience and be very careful until we found out for sure. We rode in silence the rest of the way home with little else said.

We didn't chance stopping by the house on the way back to Pastor Chuck's.

Once we arrived and had all the supplies in the house, the pastor started the task of making phone calls. Of all the people on the list, people he said he had known for a long time and people he had trusted, there was one name that jumped out at me. It was a name that had been branded in my memory from when we lived in the city. Walter Andrews was the name, but most people who knew him simply called him Walt.

Walt was one of the men from the church we attended occasionally when we lived in the city. He visited our home quite often the last few months before we moved. He came over late at night to help load the moving trucks and drove one of them to our new home. Mom and Dad had grown to love and trust him. Then we find out he had a connection to the pastor as well. Walt just may be the one with pertinent information and the answers we had been in search of on that day.

As it turned out, no one was there so the pastor left a brief message simply asking for a return call.

It was getting late and we had chores to do, so Adel fixed supper while Jeff and I did our chores. Pastor Chuck continued on with the phone calls until supper was ready. It had been a long day, so after dishes were cleaned, we each said our good nights and retired to our rooms. For myself, I was out when my head hit the pillow.

Friday, March 30

We woke up with the realization that it would be the last weekend of spring break. On Monday, school would resume and yet we had still so much to do. I couldn't believe that it had only been one week ago when the whole thing started.

At breakfast, we discussed whether Jeff and I would be returning to school and what our story would be if there were any questions about our break. We all agreed that we didn't want officials to know anything about this past week's events, not just yet.

Afterwards, Pastor Chuck and Adel announced that we would be going out of town to "get away" for a while. They told us that they felt we needed to take a break from all the chaos of the last week. They reassured us that it would do us good and that everything would be fine. We would be leaving before lunch and return early on Sunday. Jeff and I went to our rooms and packed a few things for the trip.

Before leaving, all of us made a trip to the cave at Pastor Chuck's request. He explained that we needed to leave things to look as if they hadn't been used for a while, just in case someone should stumble on it while we were gone. It was decided that we should walk so that Pastor Chuck's vehicle would not be at the house, plus it would do us good to get the exercise.

When we arrived at the cave, Pastor noticed our map hanging on the wall and asked to see it. He said that it looked too modern and would look out of place if someone found the cave, so we took it down and gave it to him. Jeff and I always thought it to be an old relic and never gave it a second thought, but when Pastor took hold of it he started examining it with an obvious look of interest. He looked at it front and back and kept making questioning, humming noises as he studied it. Jeff and I dropped what we were doing and started paying close attention to the pastor and the map he so intently studied.

Little did we know at the time that the key found in the envelope from Mom and Dad and this map were vital clues our parents had planted. We wondered if this would change our plans of leaving town or it if meant that we should take it with us and try to learn more about what it meant.

Pastor Chuck continued to study the map and turned it over once again, only to notice something had been written on the back side. His eyes squinted and his face scrunched up as if he were trying to pull something up that had been stored in his memory. Suddenly his eyes opened wide, and he snapped his fingers in response to his recollections then shouted," We need to get back to your parents' house now!"

At the excitement in the pastor's voice, we took off at a faster than normal pace toward the house. Upon our approach to the house, we kept our eyes open for unknown vehicles or anything that looked out of place. We circled the house to check things out, the same way Jeff and I did the first night. At the pastor's signal, everyone but Adel approached the house. She stayed in the cover of the woods and kept an eye open for anything unusual. That way, she would be able to warn us.

Jeff went to check the answering machine while the pastor headed for Dad's study and I wandered around the house in deep thought. I noticed the corner of what appeared to be a business card, lying on the floor and partly covered by the ruffle at the bottom of the couch. As I reached for it, there came a screech of excitement from the study. I hurriedly picked the paper up, noticed it was a calling card, and stuck it in my pocket then hurried to the study without another thought of what was on the card. As we headed to the study, Jeff told me that the answering machine had been erased. Stepping through the doorway of the room, we found Pastor Chuck opening a hatch-type door that was covered by the rug where Dad's office chair had sat.

In all the years we lived there, we never knew there was a basement in our home. We closed the hatch behind us and headed down the stairs. None of us were prepared for what we would discover as we walked down the stairs to check it out. There in the big room were supplies of all kinds for surveillance and detective work along with weapons of various kinds. Across the room was another door, but it was locked.

Pastor Chuck pulled the key out of his pocket and inserted it into the key hole. With one turn, the door opened and we followed the pastor into the darkened room. As he felt the wall for a light switch, I whispered to Jeff in a shaky voice, asking him the same question I believe he was asking himself, who were these people we called Mom and Dad?

At that moment, the light came on, and to our surprise we saw a wall with family photos as well as single photos. Not our family photos, but other people's family photos. Beside each family photo was a single photo of a child and beside that was a name and two dates. What could this be? Then, to our horror, we spotted a picture of our parents when they were younger. In Mom's arms was a baby, but I knew it wasn't me or Jeff, so the next question was, who was this child? Beside the family photo was the single photo of the child and beside it were the name Bella and the dates November 30, 1991 and September 1, 1992. The girl did resemble both Jeff and myself, so who was she and what had become of her? Could it be that we had an older sister we were never told about? What did all the dates by the single pictures represent? I got goose bumps all over my body and started to feel somewhat lightheaded at the thought of having an older sister we were never made aware of. I started to feel like we were cheated out of knowing someone who was part of our lives even though she…Then the thought occurred to me that she may be dead and that the pain…oh, could it be that the pain was too much for our parents, that they were waiting until they themselves healed from it all to tell us?

Pastor Chuck directed us to the desk that was in the room opposite the wall of photos. There were several boxes of files behind the desk, but then we discovered a journal on the desk as well as a photo album with the name Bella written on them. Taking them both from the desk, Jeff and I sat on the floor and slowly turned the pages of the photo album that told a story of our parents, before we were even thought of. With grief filling our hearts and tears in our eyes, we looked through the photo album and wondered what it would have been like to have known her—Bella, our older sister. Pastor Chuck searched the rest of the room as Jeff and I looked through the pictures of a family that had somehow become strangers to us.

Pastor Chuck found yet another door and it too was locked. He used the same key to open it, but he found that the door, instead of opening to another room, opened to some sort of passage. He suggested that we bring the books and follow him.

There were lights along the tunnel that let off a very dim glow, but it was enough to show the way. It was hard telling where this tunnel would lead as it took a couple of turns and seemed to go on for ever. Eventually we came to a staircase and another hatch door. We opened it very slowly and realized that we were now in the storage room of the old barn.

We put things back in place and turned the lights off then went to where we had left Adel. I grabbed one of the canvas bags that Mom had always used for grocery shopping and put the album and journal in it to carry back to the parsonage. Back at Pastor Chuck's house, we studied the pictures and started reading the journal. We probably wouldn't be going out of town after all.

As we started through the journal, we discovered that we did in fact have an older sister whose name was Bella. She would have been fifteen years old last November, but she had been abducted a little over two months before her first birthday. Our parents had been devastated as they searched to no avail.

Mom became very sick the years following the tragic loss of Bella. She blamed herself even though it wasn't her fault and there was nothing she could have done different to prevent it. We noticed that Mom had written a poem in the journal. I believe that all her ability to write had helped her cope and gave her a beautiful way to express herself. While reading her writings, I could sense that God had truly given her this gift.

> Dedicated to our dear Bella and all the other children who have gone missing. Bella, we love you and will never give up searching for you.
>
> Missing
>
> Calling out your name
> Are my words lost in space
> Every day I search for you
> Filled with memories of your face
>
> It's been so long ago
> Yet I'm holding tight to hope
> Not knowing of your fate
> At times I can hardly cope
>
> No body yet is found
> That matches that of yours
> We need to teach all others
> To heed the monster that lures
>
> I pray each day for your safety
> That I may hold you once again
> And for each one who is missing
> A safe return from where you've been
>
> > Love,
> > Mom

Jeff had read the poem aloud to us and there wasn't a dry eye in the room. Of course this seemed to be part of our daily bread since the start of spring break. It certainly was an emotional time in all our lives.

In the journal dated November 1, 1994, Mom wrote:

> I have suffered with awful nausea for several months and not keeping food down for nearly a month now. Sam took me to our family doctor thinking that I may need to be on medication to help me through the anniversary date of the loss of Bella. However, to our surprise, we learned that I am pregnant and my due date is March 29.

Jeff and I looked at each other as if to read the other's thoughts. Then I smiled and nodded my head in agreement when he spoke the words, "Wow, yesterday was March 29!" We often did this, and I have always heard that this was a common thing for twins. We are always finishing each others' sentences and know what the other is thinking.

Jeff turned the page and continued reading Mom's journal.

> I have lost weight due to not eating right and not keeping what I do eat down. My doctor put me in the hospital for three days to get much needed nutrition in me and help with the nausea. Today the doctor actually tried to talk Sam into convincing me to terminate the pregnancy. We both believe that life is a sacred gift from God. Both Sam and I choose to allow our children a chance at life. This is such a difficult time for both of us that I don't know how we will handle this

pregnancy, but somewhere in my heart I know that this is meant to be. I know that God has a plan for all life and he will help us through this. I refuse to sacrifice your life for the sake of saving mine.

Later in the journal, we read where they found out that Mom was going to have twins and how they decided on the names they picked out for us.

"Jeff, we are truly fortunate. If it were up to the doctors, we wouldn't be here today. I am glad that God chose them as our parents and that they protected us at the possible cost of Mom's life."

"Kylie, this makes me realize how much we are loved. It makes me long even more for Mom and Dad, so I can tell them how much I appreciate them."

We took a break from reading as Adel prepared for us an ice-cold glass of milk along with some of her delicious homemade chocolate chip cookies. After the break, Jeff read more of the journal to us. Now mom wrote as if she were telling all these things directly to us.

Your Dad moved us away from New York to Palm Springs, California, after you were born. He had hoped it would help us move on as it seemed the police had given up hope of finding Bella alive, plus I was so worried about losing you in the same way that it caused a lot of stress in our lives.

I soon discovered that your dad had never given up on finding his baby girl, your older sister, and after the move I joined Dad in continued efforts to search for Bella.

Your Dad and I are both in agreement that
we will wait until you are older to tell you about
Bella.

"Whatever that means!" Jeff muttered.

As Jeff continued to read, we found out that Dad
was still an attorney. Their efforts to find Bella lead to
the search for other missing children as well. It wasn't
long before they discovered that there was a business in
abducting children both for adoption and for exploitation
purposes. It didn't seem to matter to those monsters what
the fate of the child was as long as they got their money.

It was a short time before Mom and Dad realized that
they were putting their lives as well as ours in danger.
These people didn't want their dirty business exposed
and, as some were in fact exposed, the threats started.

There were brave people who joined in the efforts to
rid the world of this sort. They had called this organization
CAP. We didn't know what this stood for but these were
some of the people who helped Mom and Dad keep us
safe. Many of these people had become very close to our
parents, and from the information we were reading, the
organization was not a small one.

In the search for Bella, Dad found out that his own
law firm partner and friend, Terrance Hubb, from New
York, had been arrested and was involved in this human
trafficking ring. Everything began to fit in place as to
how this man had taken their Bella from them without
much effort as well as make her vanish into thin air.

Dad helped put Terrance in prison for life, but it
didn't bring Bella back home to them. On the day of his
sentencing, Terrance had been heard by many people

telling Dad, "I'll be in touch. You and your missus will always be looking over your shoulders. I know that you have two other children and you had better keep a close watch on them."

I had chills go up my spine, and it felt as if my hair was standing on end after reading the threats that spewed out of that man's mouth.

After reading the journal, we decided to return to the house, but this time we would enter through the barn. It seemed to be a much better way to go unnoticed. We would go first thing in the morning and have Adel keep a watch from the loft of the barn.

Jeff and I had a lot to digest with the knowledge of having an older sister who may or may not be alive and all that our parents had kept from us. We had such mixed emotions but Pastor Chuck and Adel encouraged us not to judge our parents too harshly about not telling us everything. Adel said, "They have both suffered a great deal and they were only doing what they thought best."

After eating a light supper, we gathered to read the Bible and each of us prayed asking for the Father to lead us. We then retired to our rooms to try to rest for the night. Before I finally drifted off to sleep, I wondered what it would be like to grow up with our older sister. There were a myriad of questions that ran through my mind. What color of hair does she have? Is it straight or curly? Short or long? Does she look like any of the rest of us? Would she be tomboyish like me, or is she Miss Prissy? Most of all, has she been well cared for or...? I was so exhausted, yet I struggled with all the things going through my mind when I suddenly remembered the business card that I had stuffed in my jeans pocket earlier.

Not wanting it to be put in the wash, I dragged my body out of bed and pulled it out of my pants pocket. It was a business card that read "JB & Sons Auto." I laid it on the dresser thinking I would look at it more closely in the morning. I finally closed my eyes in sleep, not wanting to think much about anything bad happening to Bella, so I whispered a prayer asking God to look after her then I finally drifted off to sleep.

Saturday, March 31

The Deters had spent part of their night discussing our schooling, and we found out at the breakfast table what they had decided. Our parents had set it up for them to have guardianship of us when we first moved here so there would be no problem with them pulling us from school should the need arise. They would be contacting the school Monday morning and letting them know that we would be out of school for an undetermined amount of time. We would be homeschooled for a time, which we were glad for. This would keep us from being questioned by our friends at school about our spring break.

After breakfast was over and the chores were finished, Pastor Chuck took us back to the house, but all we found was more on Mom and Dad's involvement with CAP. There was no information that would tell us where our parents would be. It seemed that all we could do then was to pray, so right there in the secret office I said the prayer that my aunt Jane always said when she couldn't find something. "God, I pray that you help us find what we are looking for, for we know that nothing is hidden from the sight of God."

We continued to pray and search, believing in the prayer that nothing is hidden from God and that he would point us in the right direction of what he wanted to reveal to us. It wasn't long before Pastor Chuck noticed the edge of an envelope hidden under the large calendar on the desk. He picked it up, saw that it was postdated Tuesday, March 12, opened it, and started reading aloud: "Terrance was placed in the witness protection program several years ago because he has agreed to help break up the human trafficking ring that he has been associated with. He was placed somewhere in Ohio where he is going by the name Jake Barns."

The officials weren't obligated to tell Mom and Dad about allowing Terrance out of the witness protection program. Receiving this letter explained why Dad had been on edge for the past couple of weeks. We prayed that Terrance hadn't harmed our parents.

Our immediate thought was, if our parents knew of this information on Terrance, what would keep others from finding out about it?

Pastor Chuck read on. "They will be keeping a close watch on him in case he tries to run. He was very anxious about the arrangement due to the violent nature of his former associates. This spring break, you may want to take the children and get away for a bit. This may be a good time to talk with them about Bella and all that you are involved in. My prayers are with you all in of this, and if I can be of assistance, please don't hesitate to call."

Pastor Chuck paused then he cleared his throat and said, "Your brother in Christ." Then, taking a deep breath and almost at a whisper, he said, "Walt."

We may never know how Walt had gained this information, but he must have had connections somewhere.

Pastor had, in previous days, tried to contact Walt. Now he was sure Walt would have some information regarding all that had happened.

His contacting Walt proved to be an unsuccessful effort, which led us to believe that he may very well be with our parents. We thought this to be a good thing though, for Walt was a wise upstanding man who loved the Lord and the three of them calling on God would be even better than two.

We may not have known where Mom and Dad were at the present, but at least we were sure that they were not alone. Whether they were with Walt or others from CAP, we were sure of one thing: the Father had sent his angels to keep watch over them.

We knew that it would be a fruitless effort to make a trip to Ohio. It would be a precious waste of time as we didn't even know exactly where to search. It would be as wasteful as chasing after the wind. There was no way that we would be going to Palm Springs either, but we couldn't just sit around and wait. We all headed back to the pastor's house for lunch. Afterwards, we all decided to take a nap. The recent days had been so stressful and the days ahead seemed to be filled with much uncertainty, so we decided to rest for a bit.

Jeff and I climbed the steps to the rooms where there were welcoming beds to collapse into. It must have been an hour or so later that I woke from my nap and remembered the card I had left on the dresser from the previous day.

I jumped out of bed and headed for the dresser to retrieve it then turned back to sit on the edge of the bed. I looked at the card, not really expecting much, but my heart jumped into my throat when I realized what was on the back of the card. I let out a holler without thinking of waking the others, but they all came running into my room in what seemed seconds.

The look on my face must have concerned them as I just sat there staring at the note. Jeff sat beside me on the bed and slowly took the card from my hands. Then he started reading it aloud.

> Your daughter was adopted by Dr. Rod Felt and
> his wife who live in Oak Hill, Ohio.

That's all the card had on it, or so we thought, until Jeff turned it over to inspect the front side. He gasped when he noticed the partial bloody fingerprint on the front side. I don't know how I missed seeing that fingerprint, except that at a glance it looked like part of the business card. We wondered what JB & Sons was and how this card came to be under the couch. We hoped and prayed this would lead us to finding our parents, and now, our sister as well! Pastor Chuck said that we should praise God that our sister was still alive, and we did just that. Adel played the piano, the pastor picked up the fiddle, and Jeff and I joined in singing the words to an old song: "When we all get together, what a day of rejoicing that will be. When we all see Jesus, we'll sing and shout the victory."

After an hour of singing, shouting, and praising God, we retreated to the dining table to discuss our plans of what to do next. Pastor Chuck picked up the phone, dialed information, and asked for the phone number of one Dr. Rod Felt. His eyes twinkled like the first star out on a clear summer night then he scratched a phone number on the note pad in front of him.

When he got off the phone, he said, "I only got an office number, but this is a start."

Then he reminded us, "Tomorrow is church, so we will need to wait until Monday to do anything."

We agreed with what was said. That way we could also make plans for things to be taken care of while we were gone. Pastor Chuck called to talk with one of his friends from church who was always willing to take care of things in his absence.

The remainder of the day was spent packing and making sure that all the animals had plenty of food so that we could leave early come Monday morning. There was such a lighthearted feeling of praise to God, for all he had done and will do, that it was as if we danced our way through the hours until it was time to say goodnight.

Sunday, April 1

Pastor Chuck preached a fine sermon that was fitting for that day. He talked about how the Great Shepherd had left the ninety nine to go out and search for the one lost lamb. He would give Jeff and me a big smile every once in a while as he spoke of God's great love for all and how he knows our needs even before we ask. It's just that he is waiting for us to ask because he longs for that communication with us. He was nearing the end of his sermon when to our surprise the pastor asked Jeff and me to come to the front of the church. I wondered what he could possibly be doing. I nearly freaked out at the thought of him saying anything about our predicament. We got to the front and Pastor Chuck asked us to turn and face the congregation. We did so after giving each other and the pastor a bewildered look. Adel came up to the front of the church to the piano and took a seat. The pastor then announced in his pastoral voice, "I believe we have here a couple of our own flock who are one year older today."

Then he asked the congregation to stand and sing "Happy Birthday" to me and Jeff. We had been so preoccupied that we had even forgotten our birthday.

After singing, the pastor presented each of us a gift to unwrap before the church. Jeff's gift was one of a set of two-way radios and a hunting knife, and I received a Swiss watch and the second two-way radio. What a wonderful surprise that was to us.

At the end of the service, he approached one of the deacons of the church and his wife and told them that he would be taking us with them out of town for a few days and asked if they could take care of Echo and things around the church. He also asked them to keep us all in their prayers for safe travel and for God's guidance. The deacon and his wife agreed with few questions asked.

Adel had made us a special lunch with cake and ice cream for dessert.

All things were already taken care of, so we were able to pack our things and start on our trip early. I had picked up Mom's journal and the baby picture of Bella. I slid the picture inside my Bible, zipped the cover up around it, and slid the journal into my backpack. I held my Bible close to my heart and prayed as we traveled down the road.

We traveled until dusk and stopped at Ashland to spend the night. None of us had eaten much since breakfast, so we decided to eat at the hotel restaurant for supper. We took our overnight bags into the rooms— Pastor and Jeff in one room, Adel and I in the adjoining room—and freshened up then went to eat. I took the picture of Bella out of my Bible and took it with me to the restaurant. I felt the need to have it near me.

As we walked through the doors, we noticed it was a buffet style establishment and it looked like they had a good variety of food, which included fried chicken, which was my favorite along with mashed potatoes and green beans. As I walked past the buffet, I noticed a sign that said "Real home cooking. Not from a box or can."

We sat at our table and bowed our heads while the pastor gave thanks. When he said "Amen," I raised my head and noticed a lady, who looked to be at least twenty, sitting in a booth all by herself. We made eye contact then strangely she quickly looked away. There was something so familiar about her that I couldn't help but look at her. I tried not to stare, but she looked very lonely and tired and I couldn't help but feel sorry for her.

I asked Pastor Chuck if we could invite her to sit with us. He smiled and nodded in agreement then he went with me to ask her to join us. As we approached her, she hung her head and started fidgeting with her key ring as if something were making her very nervous. I spoke softly introducing myself and Pastor Chuck then pointed to where we had been sitting and said, "And over there is my brother Jeff and the pastor's wife, Adel." Then I proceeded to ask her if she would like to join us at our table.

She turned her head away from us, looked out the window, and said, "No thanks. I'm fine. I really need to leave soon, but thanks anyway." She avoided any eye contact, which was sort of odd.

I could see the reflection of her face in the window and that was when I noticed the scar along her jaw line. It triggered what seemed to be a dream-like memory in which her hair was blowing in the wind. I furrowed my brow and shook my head. I did know her from somewhere, but where?

Pastor told her, "If you change your mind, we would be glad to have you join us."

I joined in, whispering, "Yes, we certainly would."

Again she answered, "Thanks, but I gotta go."

When we turned to go back to our table, she slid out of her booth and reached down to pick something up off the floor. She turned it over and looked at it then she paid for her meal and left in a hurry. Her strange behavior bothered me, but the thought of possibly seeing our sister the next day crowded the incident from my mind. We all enjoyed our food with talk of tomorrow and all the possibilities it held.

Pastor Chuck went to pay for the meal and came back to the booth with the picture of Bella. "The cashier said that the lady we had been talking to told her that one of us dropped it, and she didn't have time to return it. She asked the cashier to give it to us when we paid."

That night before falling asleep, I could feel my heart pounding, thinking that we might well see our sister the next day and wondered…wondered about…well, just wondered about all there was to wonder about.

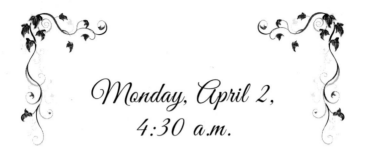

Monday, April 2, 4:30 a.m.

We woke to the sounds of sirens and horns being blown. We opened the door that adjoined our rooms. After looking outside, Pastor Chuck said he would dress and go find out what was happening. We went back to our rooms to dress and prepare to leave.

The pastor returned with some alarming news. There had been an attempted robbery at the fuel station next door and somehow a car was lit afire. Fearing an explosion, officers were asking people to evacuate the premises. The policeman and the owner had a list of occupants and were going room to room to check on people and advise them to leave. They informed the ones who had inquired that there would be more information on possible refunds after an investigation and insurance settlements were complete.

As we were loading our things, I couldn't help but think of the lady we encountered at the restaurant. I wondered if she was all right or if she had even stayed at the hotel for the night. When the last bag was in the trunk and everybody was in the car, we started out for

Oak Hill. I said a quick prayer for the lady as we left the hotel parking lot.

We pulled into Oak Hill, Ohio, and stopped at a small restaurant for breakfast. When we were seated, the waitress greeted us with a "Hi y'all, how ya doin'?" Then the pastor inquired as to the whereabouts of Dr. Felt's office. The waitress told us that they wouldn't be open that week because they had just had themselves a baby and the doctor would be staying home with his wife. He then asked, "Is this their first, or do they have any older children?"

The waitress then replied, "No, fact is they do have an older daughter. I believe she jus turned 15 las' November, but now she jus went off to that there church camp that they have in Kentucky every year for their spring break from school."

This seemed to be an open door for the pastor to introduce himself as "Pastor Chuck" from Full Gospel Country Church in Clear Creek, Kentucky. He then asked where the church camp was, explaining that he on occasion had held church camp at Grayson State Park.

The waitress smiled and stated eagerly, "I believe that there's wher' Megan went. She was in her' with 'er friends jus las' week and they were all talkin' all giddy, like girls usually do, about what fun they'd have at Grayson. This Megan's firs' time goin' to camp. I think that po' Megan was havin' a dif'cult time givin' that her ma's due any time now, and Megan bein' much older and all, but I'm thinkin' that once she gits down there she will have a blast."

When I heard the name, "Megan," my heart nearly came up into my throat and choked me. I practically yelled the name then turned to Jeff with a look of horror on my face and started to open my mouth again to speak. Jeff nudged me, stuck his tongue out, and grinned. His behavior almost made me mad until he reached down, took my hand, and squeezed it several times. I took the hint and closed my mouth only after saying ouch.

The waitress, who was talking to the pastor, seemed to have an endless number of words in each sentence she spoke. I could hardly wait until she was finished.

The waitress completed our order and headed to the kitchen. When she was out of earshot, I whispered, "The lady at the hotel restaurant. I thought I recognized her, but she seemed different. It was Megan, Spencer and Sarah's friend, you remember? Megan, the one who had stayed with them for several days a couple of years ago while her parents went to Lexington to a convention? A medical convention!"

It was all starting to make sense. I hadn't put the pieces together until now. "I believe Sarah said Megan's last name was Felt. Our sister was right there with us and none of us had a clue. People kept saying we could be sisters because we looked so much alike."

After replaying the events of that day with Megan two years ago, I was unable to keep the tears back. Knowing that I needed to pull myself together, I excused myself and Adel went with me to the ladies' room. Inside were a couple of chairs, so we each took a seat. Adel held my hand, patting the back of it as she said in a low gentle voice, "Kylie, I realize how difficult this must be for you. I see how strong you and your brother both are, and I can't help but see that God has his hand on you both. I believe through all of this he is preparing you for your calling. Just trust him and see what he will do."

I held on to these words with the belief that God would use all of this for his glory and our good. Little did I know the total impact this would indeed have on my future. I wiped all my tears then we made our way back to the table just as the waitress was bringing our food.

We ate our breakfast so as not to cause suspicion because of Pastor Chuck asking those questions about the Felts and which camp Megan had gone to and all. We figured with this being a small community, these people were probably a close-knit group of folks just like ours were. If they found out that Megan didn't actually go to camp, it may just look to them like we had something to do with her disappearance.

The pastor did manage to ask more questions about Megan and talk about the church group, camp grounds, and the local doctor. The waitress mentioned that the doctor and his family had a cabin around the Grayson Lake area. By the end of breakfast, we knew that we would be heading in the general direction we had just come from.

We stopped to get fuel at the same place we had left earlier that morning. They seemed to have had all the aftermath of the fire cleaned up, and as it turned out, the fire squad was able to extinguish the fire and keep the vehicle from exploding. We stopped at a couple of stores to pick up some supplies for the road and for camping. We needed to get a tent just in case we weren't able to rent a cabin. We realized that two hours had passed and this was precious time that we could be using to look for Bella.

We drove on to Grayson Lake, and on the way there, we all took turns calling out to God on behalf of Bella.

We had a sense that she may be in trouble and knowing that we may not be there to help her, we could petition our Heavenly Father on her behalf. We had faith that he would hear and answer our prayers.

Upon arriving at the lake, we were able to rent a cabin. This was an answer to our prayers because it was normally booked up during spring break. The lady at the ranger's office said that she just had a cancellation that morning and it hadn't been rented out yet. We bought a map of the area, which had a legend showing green dots for all the rental cabins around the lake and red for the privately owned cabins. It indicated public land and private land as well.

We drove to the location of our cabin and unloaded our things. We took the map out and proceeded to draw a circle around all the privately owned cabins. We realized that it could take us a long time to drive around the lake and back to the outlying areas where all the cabins were located. The area was known for its narrow, windy, and often rough terrain. We were able to check out a few cabins before the day ended. Pastor Chuck talked to a few people in the area to try to gain information.

At the end of the day, we were all emotionally drained and didn't feel like eating much so we just had a snack and some quiet time before going to bed.

Tuesday April 3

We woke bright and early with the hope of a beautiful and successful day. The sun was just coming up, and we could smell breakfast cooking. The aroma of bacon reminded me of the last time Mom had cooked breakfast for us. Oh, how I longed to see Mom and Dad again. I imagined telling them how much I loved them as we held on to each other crying tears of joy at our reunion.

We couldn't wait to get started on our search. Adel had already packed us a lunch for we planned on staying out all day. After breakfast, we loaded the cooler in the car and prepared to leave. We started at the farthest point from our cabin. We intended to cover as much ground as possible so the pastor and I went one way while Jeff and Adel went the opposite.

We had been out going from door to door for three hours and were coming up with nothing. We headed back to the car for lunch, and on the way, we noticed some rugged-looking people in an old, blue, beat-up Chevy van with fenders that had been partially eaten away by rust. The front headlight was knocked out and the bumper looked as if it was held on by bailing wire.

It was a wonder that the thing was even moving at all as you could definitely tell by the sound of it that it wasn't hitting on all cylinders.

They drove by real slow, and I got a good long look at the passenger. He wore a dirty, red-and-black, tattered flannel shirt with the sleeves rolled midway to his elbow. His hair was a tangled mess and he looked as if he hadn't had a bath or a shave in a good long time. The sunglasses he wore were so scratched it made me wonder how he could see out of them and why he bothered to wear them at all. I saw the passenger smack the driver on the shoulder then point at me. They kept staring at me in a way that made me want to run and hide. My body had icy goose bumps from top to bottom and my legs felt weak. I could feel this evil presence oozing from him as he flashed me a grin that showed a mouth full of rotted teeth.

I could tell the pastor felt that same presence as he quickly took hold of my hand and directed me to the other side of himself away from view of the penetrating stares. Pastor Chuck is a rather tall and broad man and this was like putting a wall between me and a predator. A wall which I was thankful for. A wall of safety.

They drove on, hooping and hollering and acting all crazy like they had had too much to drink. Pastor Chuck turned and asked if I was all right to which I said, "Yes," but the quivering in my voice told another story. He asked if I wanted to call it a day and go back to the cabin. I told him, "No way!"

Another hour had passed and we all made it back to the car to exchange information and ideas on what we were to do next. Adel retrieved our sack lunches out of the cooler, and we all nibbled on our sandwiches halfheartedly after the pastor gave thanks for the food and asked the Lord for success in finding Bella.

Before we had even finished eating, the pastor announced, "The best thing to do is ask the Lord where to look for Bella, after all he sees and knows all things."

Adel prayed, then the pastor. He finished, and at the same time that he said "Amen," his phone started ringing. He answered it without looking at the caller ID so it caught him off guard when he heard Walt's voice on the other end.

We could tell that the pastor was extremely excited, and we could hardly contain our curiosity while listening to the one-sided conversation. At first, the pastor had a twinkle in his eye then in an instant it turned to a look of deep concern.

All we could hear was, "Walt! We've been trying to contact you. They are! Good. Yes. Yes. Okay. An old, beat-up Chevy van? The north side?"

Shivers ran cold up my spine once again as I recalled the type of characters who occupied that van.

Then the pastor, in a loud voice, said, "Hello...Hello... Walt, are you still there?"

The connection had been dropped, but not before the pastor had received the news that Mom and Dad were with Walt, that they were on their way, and that Bella was in the area but could be in trouble. Walt was just starting to give directions as to Bella's whereabouts when the phone lost its signal. The only part he was able to get was that the Felt's cabin was in a more secluded location on the north side of the lake.

Without hesitation, we piled into the vehicle and drove north to the farthest cabin indicated on the map.

The terrain was indeed very rough, and we had to take it slow, which was agonizing for all of us. Upon arrival at what we believed to be Bella's location, the four of us got out of the vehicle and started for the cabin.

The pastor stopped us and asked Jeff and Adel to wait at the vehicle with the phone and keep their eyes and ears open while we went to the cabin.

On the way, I asked, "Pastor, what did Walt say that was so disturbing?"

Pastor replied, "We have to trust God that all will work out for the good. Why do you ask?"

"I noticed your facial expression while you were talking with him. There was that same look of concern you get when you give an announcement at church of a member being close to death."

"Well, Kylie, you certainly do take notice of details, don't you? God has given you a special gift, and we will have to sit down to talk about this sometime soon."

The pastor totally skirted the question and changed the subject. Deep inside, I knew that he wouldn't tell me everything that was said. I respected that and accepted the fact that he might have been trying to shield me from some ugly things, so we walked the rest of the way to the cabin in silence.

We stepped onto the porch of the cabin. As the pastor raised his hand, making a fist to knock on the door, it suddenly opened and there before us was a young, rugged-looking man. He was clean and appeared to be friendly, but you could tell by the look on his weathered face and in his muscular structure that he had lived the life of an outdoors man.

"I am Pastor Chuck Deter and this is Kylie."

"I am Jacob Brooks. What can I help you with?"

"Well, I believe we are lost and wondered if you could give us directions."

He welcomed us into his home. As I stepped inside the door, I noticed that the place was small but had a comfortable homey atmosphere. I heard the crackle of the logs being burned in the fireplace, which had a rifle hung over the mantle. I could smell the aromas of fresh baked bread, coffee, and apple pie. I could hear children singing and giggling. I thought to myself, *What a peacefully serene place to live in.* Just about then, a woman emerged from the kitchen, drying her hands on a towel.

As Mr. Brooks turned to face his wife, he said, "This is the darlin' waff, Abby."

I could see by the glow on his face as he introduced her that he was in love with Abby. I watched as he slid his arm around her and drew her in close to himself then leaned down to give her a gentle kiss on her forehead.

Pastor Chuck said, "It's nice to meet you ma'am. We apologize for interrupting you all, but we are looking for the Felts' cabin. We got lost driving all over these parts in search of it and would be obliged if you could give us directions. We followed the path from the main part of the lake, but all the windy roads got us lost."

"Is there a problem, Pastor Deter? That sweet young 'un of theirs, Megan, she usually babysits for us when they are in the area. The Felts, now them there are some good folks. Why, that Doc Felt made special trips out for the delivery of each of our four young 'uns."

The pastor just nodded his head as if to agree and show that he was listening.

Jacob said, "Why that daughter of theirs was right here helpin' her daddy with the delivery of our last baby, and I just think she may well faller in his footsteps as a doctor."

We listened as Mr. Brooks told a couple more stories of the Felt family. Then the man went on to tell us, as if he had forgotten all about his earlier question, if there was a problem, and that if we had taken a wrong turn, we would have to backtrack two miles to where there was a fork in the trail. We needed to take the west trail and drive about three more miles which would take us to the top of a small ridge with a trail back to the north. This would go on for about two more miles to where Felt's cabin was.

Jacob said, "This trail comes to a dead end, where the old Crawford cabin sits, so if you made it that far just turn around and head back to the Felts'."

The pastor thanked the man and his wife graciously, and we were on our way.

We didn't have time to waste, and even though the way was rough, the pastor did his best to hurry. Bella's life might be at stake and we couldn't risk being too late. All of us were praying. We had come this far to find her and have the chance to get to know her, so we prayed that the Father would keep her safe and that we might be able to find her.

Pastor Chuck swerved several times, trying to miss the big ruts; the small ones he didn't worry much about. As we all bounced down the road, we tried to keep our eyes open for the correct turns and possible signs of trouble. As we made it back to the second turn that would take us to the Felt cabin, I noticed something coming at us through the woods. It appeared to be kicking up dust here and there.

I strained to see it, but with all the jostling from the ruts, it was hard to make out just what it was. I finally yelled as I pointed to the black object that sped our way. "Stop! What is that?"

I felt my body surge forward as the vehicle came to a sudden stop at the edge of the narrow trail. When my body was no longer in motion, I was able to focus on the object. To my surprise, I finally saw a person on a motorcycle. Astraddle the cycle was someone with long dark hair trailing behind as if being forced to tag along.

The question that crossed my mind was, why weren't they wearing a helmet, especially if they were going to ride like some sort of daredevil? Maybe they had a death wish or something. Or maybe they were in trouble and didn't have time to think of the helmet.

As it got closer, I noticed that the person on the cycle was a girl. Then I realized it was Bella. Without even thinking, I screamed, "Bella, dear God, it's Bella!" About that time, I noticed her take a quick look over her shoulder, and deep within myself, I knew she was in trouble.

I rolled down my window and started screaming, "Bella...Megan!" I screamed over and over as loud as I could. Adel put her hand on my arm as Pastor Chuck started honking the horn. We looked ahead of us and noticed the dilapidated van coming our way. Anger quickly surged through my body like the rushing of flood waters. We heard the sound of gun fire and immediately became concerned for Bella's welfare as well as ours.

Adel picked up the phone and prayed that there would be enough signal to be able to call for help. She quickly pushed 911, and I could hear the phone ring which brought comfort to my shaken mind and body. The people who were in pursuit of Bella were so engrossed with chasing her that they didn't even notice us sitting alongside the path. Adel said, "Ma am, we have an emergency here. We are on the north side of Grayson Lake close to the Brooks cabin. There is an old, beat-up Chevy van with a couple of rough looking characters in it who are chasing a girl on a motorcycle. They just discharged a firearm."

There was a pause then Adel continued, "They are both headed in the direction of the Brooks cabin and we intend on following them."

There was another pause then she replied, "Well, I don't think that my husband will agree with that, ma am. I know it is dangerous, but you see, we don't intend on just doing nothing. If we do that, it may well be too late for the girl they're chasing."

Adel finished with, "Okay, we thank you and we appreciate your help."

When Adel hung up, she told us that the people who were chasing Bella were wanted for the fire and attempted robbery near the hotel that we had stayed at. The police had been searching the area due to reports by citizens of the van and its crude occupants. Adel said these people were considered armed and dangerous.

She added, "But we've got God on our side and we can't just sit here." And with that, she called information for the Brooks' phone number. She wrote down the number as she received it. Adel immediately dialed the Brooks home.

"Mr. Brooks? This is Adel Deter. You gave my husband directions to the Felt cabin. Well, there seems to be some trouble and we wanted to make you aware, so that you can keep your family safe and possibly help Megan out."

There was a long pause then Adel continued. "There is a girl on a dirt bike whom we believe to be Megan. If it is Megan, we believe she is heading your way. She is being chased by some dangerous men in an old Chevy van. They just passed us on the road and we are turning around to head back that way. Is there anything we can do to help?"

Adel paused for a long time and all she said was, "Yes…Yes…Okay…I understand."

While she was talking, I took Bella's baby picture out of my Bible, held it close to my heart, and started praying. When I finished, I pulled the picture away from my heart and gazed at it as if to study the face of the little girl. I noticed in the picture that Bella had a strange looking earlobe; I recalled the time when Megan had told me that it was a birthmark. I remembered the laugh we shared about it and then I smiled and whispered,

"You are almost home, Bella. Hang on. God will protect you. You are almost home."

Pastor Chuck turned the van around and headed back toward the Brooks cabin. He had only gone about a mile to an intersection when we were met by the park ranger who told us to stay put because there were guns involved. We heard sirens several minutes before the rescue squad truck and four police SUVs flew by us. We weren't at all surprised at the sound of a helicopter that flew overhead with the hospital sign on the underside of it.

Thirty minutes had passed and Pastor Chuck couldn't take any more of the waiting, so he slowly headed toward the Brooks' cabin, hoping that we wouldn't be stopped by an officer. By the time we got there, one person was being loaded in the ambulance on the stretcher with a sheet partly covering him, and one person was being handcuffed and put into the back of a police SUV. I noticed another officer with a dog heading down a trail in the woods.

As we got closer, there was a man in a uniform who held his hand up for us to stop. Pastor Chuck pulled off the roadway and turned the engine off. The officer approached our vehicle, and the pastor rolled the window down. They spoke for a moment, but I was too focused on Bella to pay any attention to the words they exchanged. After they spoke, we were allowed to exit the vehicle, cross the crime scene tape, and make our way to where Bella and the others stood.

As we walked toward the group of recently familiar faces, I noticed that the news crew had made their way to the scene. All the things that had happened for the last fifteen years of Megan's life could possibly be on display for the whole world to know. I wished that we could just be ordinary people and have our privacy.

When we reached the crowd of people, I noticed Megan and our eyes locked. We moved toward each other and this would be the first time I embraced my older sister. She had no idea and I didn't know how to tell her. We held on to each other so tight and she whispered, "Thank you" in my ear. Then without warning, she pushed me away and stared off toward the road. I turned to see what had caught her attention and that was when I noticed Mom and Dad walking toward us with Walt. I grabbed Jeff by the arm and spun him around then we both took off at a dead run toward our parents.

Through a
Mother's Eyes

Friday, March 23

I woke up at four that morning, went down the stairs, started the coffee brewing, grabbed my Bible, and headed to the old barn. In the barn loft was where you could find me most mornings at that time. It was my secret place, where I went to get away from the busy things of life and spend some quiet time with God. I often jotted down my thoughts in my Bible and underlined many of the scriptures that had helped me through the past fifteen years.

This morning as I ascended the ladder, there was a sense of heaviness, almost as if something were trying to keep me from reaching the top. This triggered an urgent feeling, maybe some sort of warning. It was indescribable, but I was able to push through and reach the top of the loft.

Once in the loft, I opened my Bible to read. Feeling a continued sense of urgency, I cried out to God as one would during a time of helplessness. It was as if I were in hard labor and praying for a safe delivery of a new life.

Lately, things of the past seemed to have found their way back into our lives. It caused a lot of undue tensions for the children, and I didn't know how much longer we should keep some of these things from them. This creates a burden for them as they are growing older and we have been gone more frequently. We may soon have to tell them the whole story for their understanding and protection. Maybe Walt was right. Maybe this would be a good time to talk with our children and let them know what this elephant in the room really is.

While in the loft, I wrote another poem. Writing was one of the ways I was able to keep my sanity through all the ups and downs of life. I knew that my Heavenly Father had given me the ability to write, and I wanted to use it to glorify Him. I figured it was a way to show others what he was to me and I hoped to one day put a collection of my writings together for my children as an encouragement in their lives and a testament of God's love, grace, mercy, and forgiveness.

Journey

One day I took a journey
Where a lot of healing took place
Your Son was right there with me
I could feel His warm embrace

Many times I did stumble
Along this rugged way
I saw his hand reach out for me
He saved my life that day

He saw all of the ruts and boulders
Of the road I was to take
I had to take this road though
No, it wasn't a mistake

I had to learn to trust in Him
To get me safely through
Casting all my cares on Him
I started each day anew

Now I sing with joy in my heart
Knowing who He is
The Almighty, the Great I Am
My King Jesus lives

Before I knew it, an hour had passed and it was time to head back to the house to start breakfast for my family. I turned to take one more look out the loft window just in time to see a star streak across the morning sky with the sliver of orange just above the treetops and the rest of the starry hosts twinkling their farewell for the day. I watched in awe as the sun greeted the earth with a promise to light our world one more day. With this, I knew that my God had everything in his hands and no matter what happens on this earth, I trusted we would all be together in the end.

Something about that morning, that same sense of heaviness, the stirring deep in the very pit of my soul, had suddenly transported me to the past. There was a scent or something that had triggered some memories of an earlier time, a dark time, a time of deep pain that started when we had lived in the city. Had God been trying to warn me or was I slipping into a state of paranoia?

We had moved to escape all the sadness and danger we thought we had left behind in the city, but had it followed us here as well? I had noticed that Sam had been a little on edge for the last week as well. When I tried to talk to him about it, he would reassure me that no matter what happened, God was still in control.

This deep peace in God caused me to realize just how much Sam had grown in the Lord over the last few years. I was glad for Sam's steadiness in our Father, as I still had a lot of growing to do in trusting Him after our tragic loss years ago. Yet I believe that that loss was what actually brought us to God.

I put my mind to thinking of spring break with our children in an effort to shake the heaviness that seemed to drag me into that black hollow place. It was a familiar feeling, one of paralyzing fear that seemed to swallow me up in guilt and shame. I tried to imagine how Sam and I would tell the children of Bella and what their father and I were involved in as a result of her abduction. The barn owl flying in to take roost for the day was a welcome distraction that brought me back to reality and with that I headed back to the house.

Our life had been far from what one would call ordinary, although my husband and I were doing the best we could to protect our children and give them somewhat of a normal life.

We had planned a spring break surprise for Jeff and Kylie. It had been so long since we were all together as a family that we planned to take them to Hawaii for their spring break vacation. They had grown so much and their features had changed, so we believed all would be fine. We had spent the last five years teaching them to survive on their own and how to protect themselves should history repeat itself and one of our precious children be taken at the hands of a predator.

Once inside the house, I started cooking breakfast. The aroma of the bacon filled the house and I heard Sam and the kids stirring around upstairs. Time seemed to go by so fast, and before I could turn around, Kylie and Jeff were heading out to meet the bus.

"There are snacks in your bags for after school. Have a good day and always remember that I love you both." My voice seemed to trail off into the air, but later in the morning, I would recall those very words and think to myself, *Were those the last words my children will ever hear from my lips?*

After the children left for school, Sam and I started packing and loading the car with things we would need while away. We had some last minute things to do as well, including getting hold of Pastor Chuck and Adel and letting them know of our surprise trip. We had scheduled a private and confidential flight with an old friend whom we trusted with our lives. He was the one who had led us to Christ after years of showing us his great love; his name was Walt. Walt also played a vital part in helping us move to Kentucky and keeping us safe in the transition from the city to the back woods.

We had asked Walt to keep all the flight plans under wraps, and we knew he would, for he understood our situation I believe even more than we did at times. He knew that things could change at the drop of a hat, and we had discussed the plans should we not show for our flight.

We had been out in the barn working and came in for lunch. It was about noon when Sam retrieved *the phone call* from the answering machine—the one that would change our plans as well as our lives. We didn't have time to call Pastor Chuck or anyone for that matter. We had to do a clean sweep on the house. That was when we rid the office and the house of all the pieces of evidence we had worked on over the years and which told our story, and took them to our secret place.

My heart started pounding in my ears and adrenaline rushed through my body as I recalled the times when we still lived in the city and how dangerous things had become for the children. The visions of the many times I had rushed the children out the back door to the "neighbor's house" to escape danger came rushing through my mind like a freight train being derailed.

Sam noticed the panic that seemed to control my body and reminded me that Our God was in control now, and he started quoting scripture. "What Satan intended for evil, God will turn to good." "The Lord is my rock and my salvation, whom shall I fear." And he started singing to me, "We shall overcome by the blood of the Lamb."

As I began to relax and focus on what my husband was saying, I realized that God had blessed me with a good man, three beautiful children, and a wonderfully supportive church family. I believed that we would make it through yet one more rough crossing and grow that much closer to God in the process.

In our endeavor to finish our clean sweep of the house, I thought of the map that Sam and I had planted in Kylie and Jeff's secret cave. We had tried to make it appear to be an old relic in hopes they wouldn't throw it away, and if anything should happen to us, Jeff and Kylie would know about what we were involved in and that they had an older sister. One day, while visiting the cave we noticed that they had hung the map on the wall. That and the knowledge that the pastor would have the key made us certain that our planning had been successful up to that point.

The door of the house swung open with such force that we were startled.

There we stood face to face with the one person who had been our worst nightmare for the past fifteen years—the very man who had taken our firstborn from us. The man who my husband had helped put in prison for what was supposed to be a life sentence.

This man had once been a partner at the Edwards, Gross, and Gibson law firm where my husband had worked during our first five years of marriage. Terrance was the name of the monster who had dominated our lives and ended one precious young life. At least that was what we had come to believe.

Now there he was standing before us and when the shock wore off, Sam and I both realized that he was barely standing. He was as pale as could be and looked as if he was ready to pass out. Sam and I looked at each other then looked again at the man before us. There at his feet a pool of blood was beginning to form. Sam and I took a step toward him at the same time. That's when he drew his gun and we both froze in place.

The words that came from his mouth were such a shock to my ears that I fell to the floor and began to weep uncontrollably.

"I'm here to help you get your daughter back, but I need your word that you will help me in return."

With this we knew that we had to help him, for he was holding a certain power in his hands that made it impossible to refuse.

The questions started pouring out and I couldn't stop.

"Where is she? Is she still alive or is this a trick? Why should we believe you?"

Terrance looked at me as if he couldn't make out what I was saying. I saw the color drain from his face and realized that he was too weak to answer any of my questions for he had lost enough blood that if we didn't do something to save him these questions may never be answered. Sam and I exchanged nods and simultaneously said, "We promise to help you." We got the bleeding stopped and got him to our vehicle. It was then that I noticed there was no other vehicle in sight. How had Terrance arrived at our home and who else knew he was there? I slid behind the steering wheel as Sam sat in the back seat caring for Terrance.

Sam called Walt to have him meet us at the airstrip. There were no questions from Walt, only the dedicated service of a friend.

Walt and his wife, Nancy, had known what it was like to lose a child to an abductor. Their situation didn't turn out as he and his wife had prayed it would, yet they never wavered in their love or service to God and others. The verses they shared with us were some that Sam would quote to me in some of my darkest times, and even now, when things seemed disparaging, he would quote the Bible to me.

Sam and Walt knew what needed to be done and we didn't have a minute to spare. They knew that no one must know where we would be taking Terrance for medical treatment. We simply couldn't risk Terrance being found by our adversaries or having him die, for that matter. Whoever would have guessed that we would be protecting the very perpetrator who stole our baby over fourteen years ago?

On the flight, I realized what time it was and that Kylie and Jeff would be getting off the bus any minute. Tears started down my face as Sam looked at his watch then at me. We were both thinking of our children and wondering how they were doing. We had left in such a hurry that the door was standing wide open and blood was still on the floor. I heard Sam say a prayer of protection for the children and watched as the tears ran down his face, fell off his jaw, and onto Terrance.

We landed on a private airstrip and there were people waiting to assist us in saving Terrance's life. The doctors who would attempt to pull this man through were working for the same undercover agency that Walt, Sam, and I were working for. It had started when several people, who suffered the tragic loss of a child, got together and formed Community Against Predators (CAP).

It was headed by people who had a relationship with God and even though they hated what the predators were doing to children, they recognized that all people needed to have the opportunity to know God as their Savior. The people from CAP would not only work hard at catching predators, but they also worked just as hard at winning them over to serve God.

The agency would send people to the prisons and jails to target predators hoping and praying for their salvation. They realized that this was one of the most effective ways of fighting the battle of human trafficking. The more people there were who served God, the lower the crime rate would be.

The scripture that CAP used in reference to their dedication to this work is found in Titus:

> Remind the people to be subject to rulers and authorities, to be obedient, to be ready to do whatever is good, to slander no one, to be peaceable and considerate, and to show true humility toward all men. At one time we too were foolish, disobedient, deceived and enslaved by all kinds of passions and pleasures. We lived in malice and envy, being hated and hating one another. But when the kindness and love of God our Savior appeared, He saved us, not because of righteous things we had done, but because of His mercy. He saved us through the washing of rebirth and renewal by the Holy Spirit, whom He poured out on us generously through Jesus Christ our Savior, so that, having been justified by His grace, we might become heirs having the hope of eternal life. This is a trustworthy saying. And I want you to stress these things so that those who have trusted in God may be careful to devote themselves to doing what is good. These things are excellent and profitable for everyone.
>
> Titus 3:1-8 (Life Application Bible, NIV)

The night seemed to drag on forever as we waited for word on whether Terrance pulled through or not. We found ourselves praying for his recovery as well as the salvation of his soul. It was after all what God called on us to do, to pray for those who do all sorts of evil. And so we did just that.

I found myself being reminded of the scripture:

But ye, beloved, building up yourselves on your most holy faith, pray in the Holy Ghost, Keep yourselves in the love of God, looking for the mercy of our Lord Jesus Christ unto eternal life. And of some have compassion, making a difference: And others save with fear, pulling them out of the fire; hating even the garment spotted by the flesh. Jude 1:20-23

You see, we hate sin and what it does to people, but we are all commanded to love and pray for the sinner. The love of God fills us so that when it is hard in our own flesh to love someone, our Father carries us through to the place where in him this is possible. With this thought I was finally able to get a little rest before the next morning.

Saturday, March 24

Terrance had gone into surgery and made it through, but he had slipped into a coma. The doctors said that he had suffered a lot of trauma, and they were sure it was prayer that brought him through. We continued to pray for Terrance throughout the day as we received updates on his progress.

We realized that it could be days before he regained consciousness, so we waited in earnest prayer for him to recover fully. The weekend seemed to go by in slow motion as we awaited each report on Terrance. Sam and I slept at the hospital so that we would be there when Terrance did come to. I went to get us both some coffee and a few snacks, but one of us if not both were in the waiting room at all times.

We spent a lot of time praying for our children and wanting to call them, but we refrained due to the possibility of our phone being tapped. We would not risk putting them in danger. We were reminded that next week would be Kylie and Jeff's birthday. How could it be possible that we would miss that most special day? We had always made it a point to make their day special and let them know just how much we loved them. Now there was this giant roadblock that prevented our being there with them. We had considered sending them a gift through the mail, but we couldn't even risk it at that point. All we could do was love them in our hearts and hope that we would be able to see them again to let them know how much they meant to us.

Walt had rested and came Sunday evening to take our place in the waiting room. At first both Sam and I resisted. Walt said, "I promise to call you if anything changes. Now both of you are too exhausted and you need to rest up for what may lie ahead."

Upon Walt's insistence, we both conceded and got a room in the hotel across the street from the hospital.

Monday, March 26

I woke up and Sam's side of the bed was empty. My body was tired, but my mind hadn't stopped going since the day Bella was taken. Sure, there were times it took a break when I was exhausted and couldn't think of one more thing, but all in all it was a fourteen-year continuation of thoughts. I convinced my body to get up, and I groaned as I stood to my feet. I ached all over, and as I looked at the reflection in the mirror that hung on the wall across the room, I saw the person I had become. My face had aged with deep creases that had formed between my eyebrows and black shadows underneath my eyes that it looked as if I had been in a fight. I had become so thin that I looked to be malnourished. The person looking back at me looked so different that I wondered who she was. Shaking my head in disbelief, I turned to look for Sam. I found him in the bathroom sitting on the side of the tub with his elbows on his knees and his face in his hands.

"How long have you been up?" I asked him.

"Since about three this morning," he replied.

"I don't feel much like breakfast. How about you?"

Sam slowly lifted his head. "Not really hungry."

We both dressed and went for a walk to get some fresh air and clear our heads. When we returned, we sat and talked with Walt for a while, and then excused ourselves.

"Should something come up, you will find us in our room praying."

Tuesday, March 27

We woke to the good news that Terrance had pulled through and was awake but was still too weak to have visitors, so it would be later today when we would be able to talk to him. In the meantime, Walt found us and informed us that he had called for some field agents to be sent to the house to check on Kylie and Jeff.

After Walt left, I went to a quiet place to spend time with the Father. This morning, tears were streaming down my face as I was remembering the words of

Psalm 103. I prayed the words, changing them to apply to me and my family.

> I Bless You Lord, I bless you with my soul; with all that is within me, I bless your holy name! Bless you Lord, O my soul, I will not forget your benefits: You forgive all our iniquities, you heal all our diseases, you have redeemed our lives from destruction, you crown us with your loving kindness and tender mercies, you satisfy our mouths with good things, So that our youth is renewed like the eagles. You execute righteousness and justice for all of the oppressed. You make known your ways. Lord, you are merciful and

gracious, Slow to anger, and abounding in mercy. You will not always strive with us, Nor will you keep your anger forever. You have not dealt with us according to our sins, Nor punished us according to our iniquities. For as the heavens are high above the earth, So great is your mercy toward us who fear you; As far as the east is from the west, So far have you removed our transgressions from us. As a father pities his children, So you pity us who fear you. For you know our frame; You remember that we are dust. As for us, our days are like grass; As a flower of the field, so we flourish. For the wind passes over it, and it is gone, And its place remembers it no more. But your mercy is from everlasting to everlasting as we fear you, and Your righteousness to our children's children, To such as keep your covenant, And to those who remember your commandments to do them. Lord you established your throne in heaven, And your kingdom rules over all. Bless the Lord, all you his hosts, you ministers of his, who do his pleasure. Bless the Lord, all his works, In all places of his dominion. Bless the Lord, O my soul!

I praise him for he desires and deserves our praises. It never ceases to amaze me at how he has opened my eyes and heart to what his Word is saying. His mercies truly are new each and every day.

By late afternoon, we were finally able to talk with Terrance and we found out that our Bella was still alive and had been adopted by a doctor and his wife from somewhere in Ohio. I thanked God that she was adopted instead of used in a sex ring. I couldn't believe that we had quite possibly lived so close to her for nearly six years without knowing.

The couple who had adopted her was willing to pay their lawyer top dollar for a specific infant, and our daughter happened to fit the description of what they wanted in their child: female, dark hair, big blue eyes, and healthy. The lead lawyer involved in the organization would portray a loving person who just happened to know all these unwanted babies, and he would reassure his clients that he could find what they desired in a child.

The call would be made to what they called the collectors, people who searched for a specific child and abducted it. They kept the child with a surrogate mother for four weeks so that they would become acquainted with each other. Then they would present the case as a single mother who wanted to do a private adoption, stating that she was unable to properly care for the child and that she wanted it to have a better life.

The way Terrance described all of this made it seem as easy as picking up the phone to order a pizza. He went on to say that there were many people who used their service because there was less of a waiting period and they portrayed themselves as legit. All this information gave me such a sense of rage that I had to leave the room to collect my thoughts and emotions.

After I left the room, Terrance started crying and apologizing to Sam for the damage he had caused to our family, the words that were spoken at the courthouse, and the fear he caused us of losing Kylic and Jeff as well. He told us of how calloused he had become in doing the business, but that he had just recently given his heart and life to God. He was now determined to make right, as much as humanly possible, all the horror he had helped cause to families during his involvement with these child abductors.

He told Sam of the depth of his involvement, how he got tangled up in all of that, and that the root of it all was the love of money. He later told us both that if those people ever found him, he was as good as dead. He described in detail how the operation was set up, all the details of how these people worked, and gave names of people who were or had been involved. It was one of those organizations that when one gets involved, it's a lifetime commitment. If you tried to get out, you wound up six feet under. We were all amazed that Terrance was still alive and prayed for his continued protection from these people. He needed to stay alive in order to help rescue children. You could say he now had a calling in his life, which may in turn cost him his life. It was what he set in order when he chose to get involved in selling children.

Terrance had lost his own family when he went to prison for his crime. His wife had a breakdown, and for the safety of her and her children, she divorced Terrance while he was in prison. He hadn't seen or heard from them since that final day in court. He told us that he believed this was the worst part of his punishment for what he had done. He did know that his family was still alive and doing well but that he had no contact nor would he ever attempt to make contact with them for fear they would be used as pawns.

Terrance then told us that four years ago, he had agreed to work with the authorities to help find as many children as he could and that they had put him in the witness protection program. This was one year after we had moved to Kentucky. Former partners in crime had found him and that was when he decided to run, knowing his life was in danger. He had been searching and praying that he would find us to let us know our daughter was alive. His plans of visiting us, when he finally found out where we lived, backfired when Frank found out where he was. Frank, one of the hired kidnappers who would stop at nothing in order to get a job done, was who they sent to kill Terrance. He was well paid and very good at what he did. Frank was one of those people who seemingly had no conscience about "getting his hands dirty" as long as he got paid.

Well, Frank had caught up with Terrance, and Terrance found out about it a little too late. He realized that there was a vehicle coming up on his tail way too fast while driving through the hills of Kentucky. Terrance told us there was gunfire and that his tire had been hit. He lost control of the vehicle and went off the road. The final landing place of his vehicle was at the bottom of a ravine at which point it burst into flames and exploded.

Terrance gave God credit for saving his life, as he told us that he wasn't wearing his seatbelt. When the car started rolling he had been ejected, which in the end saved his life. He had caught a bullet though and was cut by a piece of glass when being ejected from the car.

Frank must not have seen Terrance's body fly out of the window and consequently mistook him for dead as he stopped long enough to scan the land and watch the car explode then he sped off. Terrance's hope was that Frank believed he was dead, knowing Frank would have found a way down that cliff had he believed Terrance was still alive.

Some time passed and Terrance was then able to check his wounds and pull his thoughts together to get himself out of this predicament. Fortunately he had no broken limbs, only cuts, bruises, a very serious concussion, and a gunshot wound, which turned out to be nearly fatal.

Terrance then told us of how he managed to make it the half mile to our house and apologized for pulling the gun on us, but he had been praying that he wouldn't die without being able to help us get Bella back. Having been a coworker of Sam's, the stark realization that it was Bella who had been kidnapped for one of his clients had weighed heavy on Terrance's heart.

Before Bella was kidnapped, Terrance had been one of our closest friends from the firm. Our families had done a lot of things together, and neither Sam nor I had any clue what he was into. After Bella was kidnapped, Terrance would go to extremes to avoid contact with us. He said that he couldn't stand the weight of guilt he felt in our presence.

Terrance went on to tell in detail how Frank had targeted Bella for the couple in Ohio and how he was certain that it would be easy to take her. Terrance remembered Frank saying it would be the quickest and easiest money he had ever made. He said that he had tried to dissuade Frank, but then he described Frank as one crazy man who, once his mind was made up to do something, would stop at nothing short of death. Terrance said that he was so deep into the organization that he feared for his own family's life should he step in and prevent Frank from taking Bella. Terrance said, "I realized the pain that I helped inflict on people when the subject of prey was my closest friend's daughter, and I had to witness firsthand what that gruesome selfish act had done to a family I cared dearly about."

At times it was like a crazy nightmare that you needed to wake up from, but that was when our Heavenly Father stepped in and reminded us that everything was in his hands. We only needed to worship him and he would draw us closer. That was when the question was forged in my heart and mind,

"If none of this tragic pain had taken place in our lives, would Terrance, Sam, or I have a relationship with God today?"

My prayer, for those who are going through things they may find impossible, is that they will turn to the Father. He will give hope, comfort, direction and strength—not only strength for the situation, but strength to forgive and see others as people who desperately need him as well. This may take time to understand, but truth is worth the time to seek out and is well worth hanging on to.

It seemed that the day had just begun when I realized it was time for supper once again.

After supper, Sam and I retired to our room where we worshipped the Father, read the Word, and prayed to close out the day. We prayed for guidance and protection for all three of our children as well as ourselves and the people who served with CAP. We thanked God for his abundant blessings and the fact that we had a new brother in Christ and his name was Terrance Hubb.

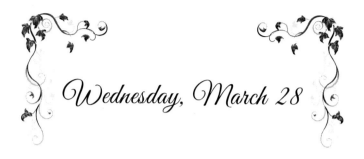

Wednesday, March 28

The day started with a devotion to our Maker then to the project of finding our daughter. During my time with the Lord, I read The Lord's Prayer and understood something in it that I had never grasped before now: "forgive us our sins as we forgive those who sin against us."

I stopped there and realized that only as I forgive others could the Father forgive me. Now that my eyes were open, I needed to forgive others so that my Father would be able to forgive me and pour out his blessings on me. His desire is to bless me, but I limit Him by my unforgiving nature. I realized just how many of our life's circumstances are very much in our control, and I realized that I needed to be very sure of my forgiveness toward others. You can say that I had had a very enlightening time with the Lord that morning.

Bowing my head, I started out saying, "Father, I forgive Terrance and all the others who are involved in this whole mess. I forgive all past offenses against me and all that may happen in the future. Forgive me of being condemning and critical of others. I desperately want to walk in your perfect love and will."

Before I could say "Amen," God spoke something else to my heart. He told me, "Ann, you know that you need to forgive yourself as well as others."

This was hard for me to do as I had always blamed myself for losing Bella. If I hadn't been so caught up in looking just right for that party the firm was having, I wouldn't have taken my eyes off my daughter.

I was at the department store picking out an outfit for the firm's celebration of a big case they had just won after nearly a year of hard work. She was in the stroller and my back was turned for only a few minutes, but that was all it took for her to be gone. There wasn't even a cry or anything. She was just gone as if she vanished into thin air.

I started by looking around to see if she had crawled out of the stroller and was on the floor. Then when I couldn't locate her, I panicked and became hysterical. Looking back on the event still sends chills up my spine and it would always be remembered as a nightmare.

It seemed easier to forgive Terrance than it was to forgive myself, but God is so merciful and full of grace and he was asking me to forgive myself for he had done so long ago.

I bowed my head as tears streamed down my face then the words came from my heart and right out my mouth.

"Father, I come to you with a broken and heavy heart. I have carried all this guilt and shame around for way too long and I now lay it down at the cross. I ask that as the days go by, you give me the strength to leave it there, never to be picked up again. I forgive myself for, for..."

I felt an arm around my shoulder and a warm hand on my hand. I couldn't open my eyes until I had finished.

Then I felt tears dropping on my hand and heard sniffling. I knew I needed to finish this prayer. I had to get it out of my mouth.

"Father," I started again, "I forgive myself for not protecting my daughter as I should have. I was consumed by my appearance and how others saw me and lost the most important, innocent being whom you had entrusted to me. I now lay all my guilt and shame in your hands. Amen."

I began crying all the more as I felt the arm around me tighten and heard Sam whisper in my ear, "I love you and it's not your fault. We will make it through this."

When all was said and I lifted my head, I felt such a weight come off my heart that there was a sense of freedom. This weight was something I had carried around and didn't even realize it until that morning. I thanked my God for speaking to me, for loving me so much that he wanted me to walk that path in life and he was right there with me no matter what. I felt I was truly able to minister to others because of his great love.

At the breakfast table, some people from CAP came together with three things in mind: to pray, eat, and discuss the days ahead. They figured we didn't have a great deal of time to retrieve Bella since things had been in such an uproar from the time Terrance had decided to leave the witness protection program. CAP figured that Terrance would be in search of Sam and me, and that his old constituents would be looking for all three of us.

Plans had to be made to find Bella and make some kind of visual contact to be sure that she was not only alive but well. Then there would be contact with her adopted parents and the assessment would be made in her best interest, whether to abruptly interrupt her life and possibly take her from all that was familiar to her or whether she would be gradually integrated into our lives. Either way it didn't seem fair. This would be very hard to do but the fact is that she wouldn't know who we are let alone know that she was abducted and illegally adopted. We also needed to consider Kylie and Jeff in the matter.

We had never told them that they had an older sister. We had put off telling them until we thought they were old enough to handle the information, since we believed her to be dead. To know that they had an older sister who had died would be one thing, but to know that she had been missing and presumed dead would quite possibly lead them to ask questions and that wasn't something we were ready to deal with.

Many details of Bella's adoption were gathered from what Terrance remembered after all these years. Following his arrest, the police confiscated all his records, but some of the records were never kept at his office and those were the ones we needed access to.

Terrance told of another lawyer, Hank, from Riley's law firm, who was part of this unsavory ring of people. To Terrance's knowledge, he was the keeper of all the adoption records, but when Terrance was arrested, he got spooked and may have moved or destroyed the records.

Upon gaining the knowledge of Hank, one of the lead agents made a phone call to New York to get agents at that end started on investigating Hank and his outfit. They would find out the location of Hank's firm and as many other details as possible before we would do anything.

Bella's records weren't the only ones that we were looking for. With all of the missing children reported, there were many others we had hopes of finding. It would be difficult for Terrance to remember all the children; therefore, we considered ourselves fortunate that he knew us. By that fact alone, most of the details of Bella's adoption were burned in his memory.

The people to whom the children were adopted out had no clue that these children were actually ripped away from their birth parents in a cruel way. It was hard to think of the adopters, the bond they have no doubt formed with the children and the pain they will suffer as well, when they find out the circumstances of the adoption. I found myself feeling very sad for them and their situations, wanting children so desperately, yet hoping that if any of them knew where their children actually came from the parents themselves would back out.

We had been in continual prayer for our two younger children for the past days. We were confident that they would know how to take care of themselves physically and could go to the pastor for help. We were most concerned about the long-term emotional affects as a result of all that had happened. Maybe we should have been more open with our children about things but that couldn't be changed now.

The fact that they wouldn't know whose blood had been spilled on the living room floor had us concerned, but there was no time for cleaning. It would have meant taking the risk of Terrance dying, and we would have never known where to begin searching for Bella or for sure what had become of her.

I had a lot of turmoil over all of this, putting one child, who was thought to be dead and wouldn't know us once we found her, over my two children who were alive and with us. But there is a bond that a mother has to her children that can never be severed, so all I want is for the three of them to be home with Sam and me, together as a family, as it should always have been.

When I had some quiet time that evening, the Lord spoke to me and from that came these words, so I grabbed my journal and started writing:

> Through all the suffering
> Through all the pain
> And everything that tears did stain
> It was Your light that showed the way
>
> Through ups and downs
> Through struggles with sins
> For who I am without and within
> It was Your grace that cleansed me
>
> Throughout the past
> Through just this day
> Whenever I get lost along the way
> Only the way of Your Son leads home
>
> Now I surrender every night
> And I surrender the following days
> Seeing my Father through His Light
> You are truly to be praised

At the end of the day, my mind was a whirlwind of thoughts and emotions, with new hope of seeing Bella soon and the aching in my heart for Kylie and Jeff. I cried out, "Father, I pray that you keep all my children in the palm of your loving hand. I pray that we will all be able to be together once again on this side of heaven. Most of all, Father, I pray that Your perfect will be done. Oh that You would keep all of the agents safe in the coming days. Guide us and help us to find the information needed to rescue the stolen ones. Give us strength to battle this evil, for our struggles are not against flesh and blood, but against the powers and principalities and rulers of this dark world. Father, I know that You have called us, Your servants, to this area to do battle and in that I know that You will be there with us."

I remember the deep sense of peace that fell over me as I was able to close my eyes in sleep.

Thursday, March 29

We couldn't help but be excited for we would be traveling to New York with Terrance to get more information on Bella's adoption and find her exact location. It would be a high-risk situation, but we were all prepared for that. Walt would be going with us and we would be meeting up with two other agents, Nick and Greg, in New York.

Nick and Greg had both served CAP as undercover agents and would be playing a large part in retrieving the adoption papers. They were lawyers who had incredible legal knowledge and persuasive negotiating techniques. They had both spent years doing undercover and investigative work, but the most important thing about them was that they both had a relationship with God.

We boarded Walt's plane and flew into New York arriving at 7 a.m. their time. There at the private landing strip were Nick and Greg, each driving a van. They pulled their vans up close to the plane and we unloaded our equipment and luggage. We had planned on being in New York for at least five days—that is, if all went according to plan.

The plan was to have Greg and Nick spend time with Terrance and gather as much information about the abductors as possible. Together with the little information we had gathered on Sunday, they would work on finding the files needed to locate the lost.

Greg would be going to that law firm to seek legal advice on adoption. Nick would be going in as the evening custodian working for the cleaning company who had been hired to clean those offices. Terrance, Sam, and I would work undercover and do surveillance from the outside. With Terrance knowing by sight many of the dangerous men working for the outfit, he would be useful as the lookout man. We had all changed our looks drastically by the usual means: haircut and dye, make-up, glasses, and the type of clothing used to make one look heavier and so on. Setting the appointments and getting Nick into the cleaning company's employee system would take some time. Part of this could be done by phone or computer, but the rest had to be done in person.

We stayed at a lodge out in the country. There was a peaceful and serene feeling as we drove up the driveway. It was there that we worked on some finishing touches of our plan. This took us most of the rest of the day, and by tomorrow morning, we would be ready to hit it. The one thing everyone working for CAP did, both to start and finish the day, was to go to God in prayer and ask for guidance and protection. So when that day came to a close, we all gathered in the living room to finish in prayer.

As Sam and I retired to our room, I couldn't help but notice the look of excitement on his face. Tomorrow would be a big day and we both had a tingling sense of anticipation about finding the information on our Bella.

Before sleep came to us, we lay in bed and talked about how close we could be to seeing our daughter once again and tried to imagine what she looked like now, what her personality and interests were and whether or not she would even accept us as family. The last thing I heard Sam say was, "The most important thing is that she is well in all aspects of her life and that she has been treated good."

Sam had fallen asleep but I lay awake with my mind unable to shut off. I decided to get up, pull out my journal, and write for a while. Getting things out of my mind and on to paper was one of the tools I used to let go of the stuff that kept my mind busy.

I usually summarized the events of the day without going into too much detail, and sometimes I wrote on things that God had shown me about myself, like where I needed to grow, what directions I needed to take, and so on. I had written for almost two hours before I decided I should shut my mind off to get some sleep. At the end of my journaling, another poem came to me.

Shadows

Running from the shadows
That follow so close behind
Trying to escape the memories
That keep running through my mind

Running from reflections
Of what use to be
Trying to outrun the shadows
That are following me

Why do I keep stopping
To look over my shoulder
Letting time pass me by
As I'm quickly growing older

What a waste it is
To not eventually see
These shadows ruin my future
As I allow them to chase after me

As I walk in the beautiful light
Of my heavenly Father
I keep my focus on Him
Then there are no shadows that bother

There is sweet peace and joy
As I walk by His side
In the light of His love
Those old shadows have to hide.

Thank you, Jesus, for shining your light on me and causing sin to have to flee.

I crawled in bed and was soon fast asleep.

Friday, March 30

That morning, as we gathered around the breakfast table, there was an unusual silence. It was a rarity for all of us to be this mute at the same time. My mind stirred and I began to shift in my chair as if I were trying to get out from under a heavy, invisible weight of great magnitude.

Walt broke the silence with a stunning question. "Have any of you sensed that we shouldn't go forward with our plans today?"

It was like dominoes as each person raised their hand and bowed their head. I almost hated the fact that I was indeed feeling the same as the others in the room. Sam was in agreement as well.

Nobody felt very hungry and we all decided to scrap our plans for the day and use that time to fast and pray. There was no doubt among the group that God had laid this upon us whether to protect us or lead us in another direction. We may never know in that lifetime.

It was a unanimous decision that we should fast and pray the rest of the day due to the extreme stirring that we all experienced that morning. We would meet in the morning for a consensus on what to do next.

Saturday, March 31

I woke up at 1:45 a.m., unable to sleep. I decided that I would go out on the balcony off our room and talk with the Father. As I sat down, the words of a song began to play in my mind. It was a song describing our love for the Father and his love for us. I started singing out loud and that was when I noticed the prisms dancing on the horizon. It was as if the Father was really dancing with me. I felt his presence so closely and intimately that I didn't want to move for fear of him leaving. I heard him say, "Follow my lead as you dance with me, and you will never miss a step."

Some time had passed and I heard the patio door open. Sam stepped out to ask if I was all right. I pointed to the beautiful display of the Northern Lights and shared with him what the Father had spoken into my heart. Sam and I stood there holding one another and praising God for his goodness.

We both were able to get back to sleep at about 4:00 a.m. and woke again at 6:00 a.m. to the alarm going off. We got up and prepared ourselves for the day. Remembering what the Lord had spoke to me earlier helped me to understand that he had perfect timing in this dance of life.

There was definitely a supernatural pull of the Holy Spirit to wait. We may never know why, but we know the One who does know, and so we will wait. One thing that we all agree on is that we should listen and do as the Holy Spirit leads.

Sunday, April 1

It had been over a week since we last saw Kylie and Jeff. We prayed that it would soon be over so that we could be home with our children where we belonged. Lord willing we would have all three of them.

Some agents had informed us that Kylie and Jeff were fine and had been staying with the Deters since Tuesday. The agents had observed them and found them to be well. Thursday they had tried to make contact at a fuel station, but Pastor Chuck had been cautious about things, not wanting harm to come to the children, so the agents left them with a calling card and let it go at that.

Our hearts broke at the thought of what they might have already endured and what they might be going through. We prayed that in time they would be able to mend, as well as forgive us for sheltering them too much.

We were also concerned about the Deters, but there were matters that needed to be kept in the dark until it was safe for all concerned. It wasn't just our family that had been affected by this ring of abductors. We were confident that the Deters would be praying about everything without being condemning or judgmental, and that the Father would guide them. They were just that reliable in their relationship with God and others.

Sam and I took time to pray at the beginning of each day, both in our private time with God and our time together with him. Understanding that he created us, and all that is, helped us to know that everything was in his hands. "He knows all" was one of the phrases that Sam and I frequently used to help us persevere in our daily lives. We were ardently thankful for where he brought us from, for what he had in store in the future, and for moments like these when we knew he would carry us through.

> And not only so, but we glory in tribulations also: knowing that tribulation worketh patience; And patience, experience; and experience, hope: And hope maketh not ashamed; because the love of God is shed abroad in our hearts by the Holy Ghost which is given unto us. Romans 5: 3-5

I believe that there is always hope in the Father, and as I continue to grow from my tribulations on this earth, he continues to pour out his love into my heart.

As we all gathered around the breakfast table that morning, we realized that Terrance wasn't there. Concerned, about whether or not he was well enough to have endured the flight and the excitement of all that was happening, or if he had spooked and bailed on us, Sam and Walt went to his room to check on him.

They reappeared a short time later with Terrance. His head in his hands and sobbing like a baby, he began to tell us that he remembered something vital about the day he showed up at our house. He knew he had lost so much blood that he might not make it, so he had written us a note on the back of a calling card.

We were unaware that the trauma Terrance suffered had caused him to forget about a note that he intended to give us. It contained the last known state and town of the doctor who had adopted Bella. That one piece of paper could be the thing that would put my other two children in danger. We had worked so hard all these years to prevent Kylie and Jeff being put in harm's way, but the decision to join CAP and fight evil had done just that.

The CAP members all came to the conclusion that the mission would be put on hold with the hopes of successfully recovering one lost child, our Bella. It was such great news, and we all needed something good to hope for. It had been a long time since we had located a loved one this many years after the abduction and there was hope of reuniting them with their biological parents.

Terrance agreed to stay with the CAP organization and continue to help with the locating and rescuing others who had been taken. This way he would be repaying his debt to society, and he would be taken care of as well.

By late afternoon, we had started trying to contact Pastor Chuck, but there seemed to be no answer. We had missed our children so much and couldn't wait to see them. We would fly home by Tuesday morning, be home to explain things to the children, and hopefully locate Bella by Wednesday. Well, that was our plan anyway.

Monday, April 2

We gathered for breakfast in the morning. Walt had tried to schedule an earlier flight, but the airport had delays due to the weather. We were now scheduled to take off the next morning, and it was so hard to wait. I had to fight back all the what-if scenarios that kept trying to burrow through to my mind causing me to not trust in God, but rather fear the worst. Sam was well aware of what was happening and prayed against the attack that I was under. We both knew that the enemy would use all things to keep us in a perpetual state of fear. In doing this, he would win the battle over our minds which would leave us unprotected.

Realizing this, Sam and I turned to our sword, the Bible, and started arming ourselves for battle as we read Ephesians 6:14-18.

> Stand therefore, having your loins girt about with truth, and having on the breastplate of righteousness; And your feet shod with the preparation of the gospel of peace; Above all, taking the shield of faith, wherewith ye shall be able to quench all the fiery darts of the wicked.

> And take the helmet of salvation, and the
> sword of the Spirit, which is the word of God:
> Praying always with all prayer and supplication
> in the Spirit, and watching thereunto with all
> perserverance and supplication for all saints.

As I read this scripture I told myself these things: We will stand and be strong, for the truth will set us free. Our hearts will be protected and we are not to fear this journey, for God's word gives us peace. We will trust God to protect us from the lies of the enemy. The helmet of salvation is my deliverance, safety and welfare. I will use the word of God to pray vigilantly and persistently.

This is a battle that is unseen by most people. We all tend to see, with external eyes, the obvious symptoms, and using our emotions we explain away what is really happening. Just listen to the news, read the local paper, or watch as your friend, coworker or fellow student loses touch with reality, hears voices, goes off the deep end, or gets a phone call saying their child has committed suicide or been murdered. It's all around us and there is only one safe place to be. That safe place is directly in the center of God's will.

I had, over the past three years, become more aware of the reality of the spirit realm. There is a war that is going on. It is a war unlike any other and it is intensifying daily. It is a war between heaven and hell, angels and demons, Good and Evil, and this war will eventually end. It matters on which side you are serving, whether you make it to a beautiful reward where there will always be peace, or you live forever in a place of great torments. The only chance we have to live forever in the place of peace depends on who we serve while here on this earth. It is our choice and the only chance to make this choice is while we are still alive here on this earth.

I am afraid that there are so many people who walk around with this veil over their eyes and mind that tells them that "as long as I am happy, getting my wants met, and there are no immediate problems then all is well and I don't have to worry about or prepare for the afterlife." Sailing smoothly without learning to prepare for the storm that awaits will eventually sink the ship.

It is my heart's desire to help people prepare, and I believe this was one of the reasons that God had allowed us to go through all that we had been through. He was preparing us for the grand finale. Since I had come to know God, I have had a desire to know his Word and communicate with him. It brought me to a place where I understood more and more that, with God in my life, my sufferings would produce perseverance, character, and hope. And I know that Romans 5:5 tells me that hope maketh not ashamed; because the love of God is shed abroad in our hearts by the Holy Ghost which is given unto us.

Along with my battle buddy Sam, I made it through yet another war victoriously. It was the battle for my mind. *A lesson learned, a battle won, now with strength in Your Son, I will carry on.* We retired the day and peacefully awaited the morrow.

Tuesday, April 3

We loaded our things into Walt's plane and took off for home. We had a bumpy ride and were glad when we landed. It was 10:00 a.m. and we still had to drive for an hour to make it home, but when we arrived, we found that the pastor, his wife, and our children were gone. We contacted one of the deacons of the church, but all he knew was that they had gone out of town and were intending on being back by Wednesday.

Walt had come with us to help out. He knew that there may be some problems with regard to getting Bella back and we didn't know how the children would react to all that had taken place. We stopped at the house and realized that it had been cleaned. We also noticed that the hatch door under the office chair had been disturbed, so we went down to check things out. It was evident that someone had been down there. We knew by the things that were taken that it was most likely the children who had been there. Our picture of Bella was gone and all the evidence, along with the journal, was missing.

We knew that Kylie and Jeff were with Pastor Chuck and his wife, but where had they gone? We figured them to have taken the things that were missing from the room and hoped that they hadn't gone off on a search for Bella. We weren't sure what kind of situation they would be heading into.

We tried to contact the pastor on his cell phone, but it went directly to a message saying "The number you are trying to contact is either out of the area or is temporarily out of service." It was almost noon and time was getting away from us, so we decided to drive to Oak Hill, Ohio, and continue trying to get through to the pastor.

We were almost to Oak Hill when Nancy called Walt. Walt was having a hard time hearing his wife but he was able to hear the excitement in her voice, so he asked us to pull the vehicle over. We came to a stop at a crossroad, and as Sam pulled over, I couldn't help but notice the wide-eyed look on Walt's face. It was a look of disbelief mixed with fear.

It sent chills up my spine, and I couldn't help but blurt out, "What? What is it, Walt?!"

He turned and said, "Nancy has been trying to contact us since she received a phone call this morning. It was a young girl calling herself Megan, stating she believes she is the girl named Bella in the missing poster. We need to ask the Father for protection for Bella.'

"But what is wrong? There's something wrong isn't there!"

Walt said, "The girl believes she may be in danger. Nancy tried to get directions from her, but the call was lost after Megan told Nancy that she was on the north side of the lake in a remote area."

I began to pray. "Jesus, I come before you and with all that is in me, I ask that you keep all of my children safe. Father, you know where Bella is and you know what her situation is and I ask that you keep your angels as a hedge of protection around our children. I pray that you give us an opportunity to know our Bella once again and that she comes safely back into our family. We ask all of this in the name of Jesus, Amen."

We drove on down the road and stopped at a fuel station in Ashland just off Highway 60. There was a hotel with a restaurant next door. Sam fueled the vehicle while Walt walked to the hotel restaurant to question people on possible sightings of Pastor Chuck, Adel, and the children. He pulled his cell phone out to try to call the pastor but there was the same message as before.

Walt received another call from his wife just before reaching the restaurant. This time, Nancy was in a bit of a panic. She told Walt that Bella could be in trouble and we needed to get to Grayson Lake as soon as possible. He got as much detail as his wife had to offer, jotted it down on his notepad, and walked on into the restaurant.

He approached the lady at the cash register, pulled out a couple of photos, one of Kylie and Jeff and the other of pastor and Adel, then began asking if anyone had seen any of the people in the photos. There was a waitress who saw Walt holding the pictures. She happened to be the one who waited on the four of them Sunday evening.

Walt thanked the lady, after telling her as little as possible about what was going on. He then turned and pulled his phone out to try contacting the pastor one more time before going to the vehicle. To his surprise, Pastor Chuck answered the phone. He had a bad connection with little signal, so he tried to get all the pertinent information from Pastor Chuck. However, he lost the signal before he was able to get the exact location of the Felt cabin.

Walt hurried toward the car and I could tell there was something urgent in his step. He hopped inside the car and told Sam to get going. Before I even got one word out of my mouth, Walt hit the redial on his cell phone. There was no answer, so he turned to me and told me that he had received another call from Nancy. When he repeated what she had told him, my heart sank and I closed my eyes in an effort to maintain control of my emotions. We all needed to be alert and quick to think at this time, so I drew in a slow, deep breath.

Walt told me to get a pen and pad out to take down some phone numbers of people he wanted me to call for help. I jotted down the numbers and pulled my phone out of my bag to begin but there was no signal. I tapped the phone, waiting for a signal as we headed down the road. I turned the phone off and rebooted it. This had helped many times before. I eagerly awaited the screen to come on and as it did, I nearly screeched for joy to see that it had three bars. I started dialing the numbers and communicating our predicament to the persons on the other end.

Walt was able to connect with Pastor Chuck again and get an exact location of the Felt cabin. He hung up and made a couple more calls. As I was hanging up with my last contact, Walt's phone rang. He jotted down some directions on a paper and wrote the name Brooks on it. When he hung up, he told Sam that we would not be going to the Felt's cabin but to the Brooks home. He explained, "That last call was Pastor Chuck and Bella was just spotted on a motorcycle heading toward the Brooks' home." He proceeded to tell us that there was a van with a couple of guys chasing her and that they had fired a gun at her.

Sam sped up as we had some distance to go to get to the location of our children and friends. Tears streamed down my cheeks, and I bowed my head thinking how close we had come in getting our Bella back. I couldn't accept the fact that she may be coming home in a coffin.

The ride was so rough in spots that I thought the car would surely wreck. However, I could feel that the hand of God was on us and it was only by his grace that we arrived at the Brooks cabin speedily and safe. Sam pulled over as close to the cabin as he could. There were already police and rescue workers at the scene as well as the news media. Two officers approached the vehicle and asked for our ID. Sam explained that our children and friends were in the group of people who were standing near the barn. We were instructed to exit the vehicle and follow the officers. They held the crime scene tape up as we ducked under, then they left us to walk to the crowd in search of our family.

Kylie spotted us first and grabbed hold of Jeff's arm, turning him in our direction and pointing. At first they both stood there as if they had seen a ghost, but then, almost simultaneously, they ran toward us. My heart ached as we ran toward each other. As we clung to our children, Sam cried out, "We love you and it will all be okay now. We are so sorry for all you have been through. We are so sorry."

We all wept and cried so loud, releasing all the emotions that had been a part of the whole ordeal. We knew that it was only the beginning of the healing that would be taking place in the days, weeks, and months ahead.

After a time, Kylie stopped abruptly, turned, pointed in the direction of the crowd from which they came, and said, "We found her. We found Bella."

Holding hands, we all walked toward Bella. Then suddenly, my whole world collapsed as I watched her legs give way and her body fall to the ground in a heap.

Strangers

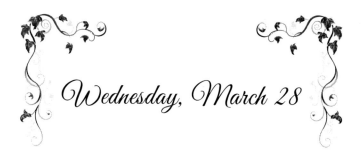

Wednesday, March 28

I looked at the beautiful leather-bound journal lying on my dresser. There on the front was inscribed "Megan Adriana Felt." It was one of the many birthday gifts I had received over the years from my parents. This journal seemed more special to me though because it contained writings of the recurring dream that I had been having the past year. I had been dreaming that I was in a foreign country without my family, but I felt very safe. There were strangers all around me, yet they treated me as if they knew me somehow. It was strange that I would feel so safe, because in previous dreams that I had I was on the run from an unknown presence that was chasing me.

I started keeping a journal when I was younger. It was one of the things that my counselor from school had me start doing when I was nine years old. A year before, I had started having these wild and sometimes nightmarish dreams. They had seemed so real that there were times when I would wander through the day thinking I was still dreaming. It affected my grades and so my parents agreed with the counselors that writing would be a good sort of therapy for me, plus I enjoyed jotting poems and such down anyway. As I looked down at this beautiful book of sorted dreams, there was an eerie reality to them all.

It had all started three months ago when my parents sat me down and gave me what was supposed to be good news. They were so overjoyed they could hardly wait to tell me that I was going to be a "big sister," which explained Mom's recent weight gain. Yes, it was true; they were going to have a baby. After fifteen long years as an only child, they decided to have another baby. They reassured me that I would always be their princess and nothing would change that, but in time, things changed beyond recognition for me.

At first it was very exciting and I could hardly wait to have a baby in the house. Yes, there was the usual stress, grumpiness, and hormonal things that some pregnant women go through. But overall it wasn't any less tolerable than other times. However, there was one life-changing day, when she was nearly due, when I overheard mom talking on the phone with one of her sisters.

She was crying when she said, "Doc and I have never given up hope of having our own child and after all this time, our dreams are finally coming true."

Mom paused while she listened. Then she said, "I know, Kathy. I would never think of hurting Megan, but I'm just so excited about making it to term with this baby."

I was stunned and felt paralyzed, hoping this was a dream and that I would wake up soon. I stepped away from the door so Mom wouldn't see me and I continued listening to her conversation with Aunt Kathy.

I could only hear her side of the conversation but it didn't take a rocket scientist to understand what was going on. She recalled all the many times that she and Dad, whom she called Doc by the way, had been expecting, only to be disappointed when her body gave way to a spontaneous abortion.

The biggest shocker was when she said, "Kathy, I will never forget the feeling of bringing Megan home from the adoption agency, but I can't wait to know what it will be like to bring *my* baby girl home from the hospital."

With that said, I turned to go to my room, not wanting to listen to another word of the conversation. My head spun with all the words that were spoken and I couldn't stop them from playing over and over in my mind. I sat on the edge of my bed, staring at the floor, trying to think of all the good times we had had as a family. I was trying to hang on to something, anything that would disprove the information I had just acquired. I put my mind to thinking of Aunt Kathy and the good times we had.

Kathy had always been my favorite aunt. She was so kind and soft-spoken, yet she had a sense of inner strength about her. When I stayed with her, she always had something that we would work on together. Things like cooking, working on a scrapbook, sculpting, or helping those in need. One thing I will never forget is how happy Aunt Kathy was when I was around. She was always humming or singing songs, and she seemed to dance where ever she went.

Kathy would always remind me of how precious I was and that if she had ever had children, she would have wanted to have a girl as sweet and beautiful as me. My aunt wasn't married and was childless, but she didn't seem to let any of that stop her from caring for others and showing them love.

She actually taught me more about loving people than my own parents ever did. They seemed to be so caught up in their social life that they didn't have time to think of the less fortunate. Oh sure, they would give during the holidays and whenever they knew they would be recognized for their contributions, but they never sought needy people out and helped them because it was the right thing to do. They instead seemed to glamour in the spotlight as the giver.

There were several times I stayed at my aunt's house when Mom would go through some tough times. Now I know that Mom had not been able to carry a baby to full term. She seemed to change during those times. It was as if she were Dr. Jekyll and Mr. Hyde. There were times she was so distraught that she would take it out on me as if I had done something to cause her pain. I wasn't sure at times whether I should hug her or run and hide.

I sat for what seemed hours on the edge of my bed wondering who I could turn to and who else was aware that I was adopted. I started to believe that this information was a very big secret, and if it ever got out it may somehow damage the Felt reputation. Mom and Dad were such upstanding citizens in our town and I was always labeled "Doc's girl," as if people didn't realize that I too had a name, "Megan."

When I was a kid, I guess it didn't bother me much, but as I started developing a sense of independence, I desired to be recognized as an individual and not an appendage of someone else's accomplishments. Now the person I thought I was, along with the security I had always known, started to crumble into a heap like a skyscraper after an earthquake.

Something my dad always used to say was that an animal who feels threatened will either fight or take flight. Choosing the latter of the two, I felt a desperate need to run from all I was facing. It was a difficult decision to leave familiar surroundings, but to me it seemed I had no choice. I felt the threat of being marked like a culled animal who had developed a disease or deformity and needed to be gotten rid of. I was, by no imagination of my own, being treated very differently by both my parents the last week before Mom's due date.

Spring break was coming up at school and though my parents hadn't spent a whole lot of their lives in church, they planned to send me to a church camp with one of my friends during that time so they could "bond with their baby." Mom was due the first weekend of spring break. I figured all this would be another distraction for them and I could pack my things with nobody being suspicious.

The last several days before mom was due was a very busy time, so I figured no one would notice that I was making plans to leave and not come back. I decided that I would take my dirt bike due south and hopefully make it to our cabin at Grayson Lake State Park in Kentucky before anyone noticed I was gone. Spring break was only one week long, so I had that much time to figure things out all on my own. I thought this was a place nobody would think to look for me as I always complained whenever we took our vacation there.

We had lived out in the country in Ohio for as long as I can remember and I loved the country life, but in my mind having a cabin even further from society was a ridiculous way to spend a vacation. I always wanted to experience the big city and all the sounds, lights, and sights, but my parents' love for the great outdoors outweighed the desires of this youngster. They had seen enough people in their tedious days of work that they just wanted to get away from it all and enjoy each other.

My dad was a well-known and very busy doctor in our little town. He would also travel to nearby towns as well, where he had clinics. Mom had been his nurse for years, but when they found out that she was pregnant this time, they decided the stress may cause her to abort again, so she quit her job and they hired a nurse in her place. This meant that Mom was home a lot more than I was accustomed to, but Aunt Kathy came out to help around the house and a maid was hired as well.

I did my best to minimize contact with Mom after overhearing her conversation with Aunt Kathy that day. She seemed perfectly fine with our lack of family time and disconnect, making it easier for me to leave. And the day was soon approaching which made me more anxious than usual.

I had saved my allowance and some money that I had earned from odd jobs for the past two years. This would come in handy for getting the things I would need along the road. In my mind, I was ready to go on this journey and be on my own with no thought of the possible trouble that was looming on the horizon.

Thursday, March 29

The lady I had known as Mom delivered her daughter today at 11:00 a.m. After I finished my chores at the farm, Aunt Kathy took me to the hospital. There was an unusual silence between us as she drove to the hospital. I sensed that there was a heavy weight on my aunt's heart. I tried to act as normal as possible, but I actually didn't have much to say at that moment. I loved my aunt but didn't want to let on, even to her, that I knew why this event meant so much to the people I had known as my parents.

When we arrived, I allowed the excitement of a new life to take up residence in the place where there was extreme pain. As we walked in the room, I couldn't help but stare at the little bundle in the bassinet. There was a label attached to it that read: Elizabeth Grace Felt. She was so tiny and beautiful that my heart leapt when I held her. I asked Aunt Kathy to take a picture of us. I wanted to have something to remind me of the good times and hopefully drown out the last few months of pain. Grace was so innocent and even though I knew she was not my blood relative, she did resemble me somewhat. This brought tears to my eyes and Kathy asked if I was all right. I managed to control myself, put on a smile, and whispered, "Yes."

We didn't stay long at the hospital so that the Felts could be alone with their daughter. Aunt Kathy and I walked to her vehicle with a deafening silence that hung in the air. I slid into the car seat then grabbed the door to pull it closed. The air was so thick with nothingness that as I gave the door a tug, I could hear every noise it made from the high-pitched screech of metal against metal to when the door made contact with the frame of the car, and finally the latch securing the door in its place. It was like having an ice-cold hug from a life-sized transformer. It sent chills up my spine, yet there was an odd sense of security in it because it was what broke the silence. As Kathy started the vehicle and pulled out of the hospital parking garage, she smiled and started humming the tune to one of her "I love Jesus" songs.

Kathy was staying with me at the farm, as arranged by Mom. She had agreed that it was easier for her to stay at our house than to drive me out twice a day to do the chores. Plus, she did the cooking for Dad and me. She cooked a week's worth of meals and froze them so that when Mom got home, she wouldn't have to cook. Aunt Kathy was always looking out for other people and that was one of the things that I dearly loved about her. She was a true servant and it was evident that she felt blessed to be able to serve and give of herself to others.

After visiting at the hospital, we went out to eat and have some "girl time," as Aunt Kathy always called it. She wanted to do something special for me so she took me shopping. She bought me the very thing I had been saving for but couldn't buy anymore what with my plans to leave.

They were a pair of new boots that I had been eyeing for the past six months. Kathy had seen me "ooh" and "ah" over them the last time we went shopping together. After she paid for them, she told me that she had planned to wait until the baby was born to get them for me. She said, "I believe you need something to remind you that you are so very precious and that I love you. You will always hold a most special place in my heart."

Kathy obviously didn't want me to feel left out. It wasn't a problem that she bought the boots for me, but if Mom and Dad had known that she was spending two hundred dollars on me, they may not have liked it so, Kathy told me, "This was our secret." I just smiled and gave her a big hug. Tears were streaming down my cheeks as I told her that I loved her and wished I was her daughter. I told her that she made me feel so loved, not because of the boots but because I knew that she was genuine about her love for others.

We arrived home and after putting my boots in my room, I headed out to do the evening chores. Kathy was cooking my favorite meal tonight: fried chicken, mashed potatoes, and green beans. My parents had written an excuse for me to be out of school for today and tomorrow. I knew I needed to spend some time on my homework after supper tonight so that it would be done before leaving for camp. Not that it mattered much except that it would keep me busy and Dad would be expecting me to work on it.

It was almost 5:00 p.m. by the time I finished my outside chores. As I was coming in from the barn, I heard Dad pulling in the driveway. I picked up the pace because Dad never liked waiting for his supper and we always ate right at five. As I cleaned up, I left the bathroom door open a bit so that I could hear Kathy and Dad talking. They were talking about baby Grace of course. Then they lowered their voices, but I did hear my name mentioned.

I eased closer to the partially opened door and heard Dad ask Kathy, "Do you think she knows, Kathy? Do you? We have to do our best with the situation and should she find out…Well, I don't want to think what the outcome would be. I am doing my best to not treat her differently. But you know the feeling of finally being able to hold my own flesh and blood and know that I took part in creating this life. It is hard to keep the two separate."

I heard Kathy reply to him in an almost harsh voice, which was unusual for her to do. "I swear, Doc, if you hurt that girl, you will have more than the law on you. She doesn't deserve to be treated the way you two have been treating her these last nine months. You need to think of someone besides yourselves for once, Doc. Really, have you even thought of what others have suffered and the fact that you chose to keep silent after you knew the facts?"

What was Aunt Kathy talking about? She seemed very upset but then I accidentally bumped the bathroom door and it squeaked which ended their conversation abruptly. They both put forced smiles on their faces like mannequins, and Dad heaved a big sigh saying, "Let's eat!"

Dad started to dig in but didn't get the fork to his mouth before Kathy cleared her throat rather loudly and said, "Shall we pray?"

Dad stammered, put his utensil down, and said with a sheepish smile, "Yes, Kathy, would you please ask the blessing?"

This was one of the things that were so different about my aunt. She always took time to pray before meals and about everything. She would always tell me that God knows all things and we should do nothing without talking it over with him first.

My parents, on the other hand, would just go through life doing whatever seemed good to them with no thought of God. They never read the Bible nor did they pray on a regular basis. The only times I ever heard them pray was when Aunt Kathy joined us for a meal and when Mom was going through her mean spells. I surely didn't understand this at all because on one hand they would pray for Mom to make it through, whatever she was going through, yet she felt it was all right to take her pain out on me. I had listened to them curse, talk bad about others, and watched them treat others unfairly just to get ahead. Their lives seemed to be all about social status with no thought of who they truly were deep inside. None of this made a lick of sense to me. Why would a person trash talk God and treat others poorly, then turn around and cry out to God for help?

After supper Kathy and I cleaned up the dishes and put the leftovers away. She would be here until Sunday morning then she planned to go home. This would help out until I left for camp. I went to my room, finished my homework, and slipped into my pajamas. Before crawling into bed, I went to tell Aunt Kathy good night. I found her in the library weeping and praying as if she was in anguish.

"Aunt Kathy, what's wrong?" I asked her. She quickly pulled herself together and smiled, but I could see the pain and I guessed that she was thinking of her conversation with Dad earlier that evening.

"I just wanted to come tell you goodnight." I told her. She took my hand and had me sit next to her on the couch.

"Megan, I was just praying and asking God to bless you. I sense that you may be feeling left out right now with the new baby and I am concerned about you."

I had to keep myself from falling apart and sharing all this pain that I have bottled up inside me. I took a deep breath, exhaled very slowly, and I said, "Kathy, I am feeling a little overwhelmed right now, but it will be all right. I believe everything will work out and in time it will all be okay."

She asked if she could pray with me before I went to bed and I gladly accepted. I knew that I would need strength and prayers to follow through with my plan. After she prayed, I headed upstairs to bed where I would attempt to sleep.

Friday, March 30

This day seemed to fly by with all the things that we had to do before Mom came home from the hospital. She would be here tomorrow afternoon, and I was glad for that because it only meant that I didn't have to spend much time here with her. The thought of being around her was working on my emotions and I had to keep them under control.

Today I felt I had to convince Aunt Kathy that I was going to be fine, so I did the best acting that I had done since having the lead role in the high school play last fall. Staying focused on the tasks ahead of us helped, and I was pretty sure that I had her believing I was fine after the day was over.

We both worked so hard on the final touches of the baby's room, and I really did enjoy doing that. There were some wall decorations that Mom and Aunt Kathy had picked out but hadn't had the time to put in their places. We hung two pictures and placed the decals on the wall just above the bassinet. At one point, I felt my emotions welling up inside of me. It felt as if I were going to burst into tears, so I would divert my thoughts by asking Aunt Kathy her opinion of the placement of the decorations.

At one point, I started to sing an impromptu song. This was one of the things that my friends and I would do just for fun. Aunt Kathy would smile, and when I finished singing, she would start in singing one the religious songs she had taught me. Of course, I would join in singing these songs as well.

By the end of the day, we had put the changing table together, set it in the far corner of the room, and put the decorations up. Aunt Kathy had washed all the new baby clothes. I helped put the clothes away then I attached the mobile to the railing of the crib. By the end of the day, we were both exhausted and I had little trouble sleeping, which was a good thing for a change.

Saturday, March 31

I was up early to get chores done while Kathy cooked breakfast. After we ate and cleaned the kitchen, Dad and Kathy headed to town. Before leaving, they asked if I wanted to come, but I declined. Dad shot Kathy a puzzling look, and before either of them could say anything, I told them I needed to get some things packed before I left for camp tomorrow. I acted all excited about camp, and they seemed relieved at my quick response. Mom would be coming home today but not until late this afternoon, so I was left alone for most of the day. Taking advantage of the time alone, I took some of my extra supplies out to the barn. I also located my key to the cabin and put it in a pocket of my backpack. By the time everybody made it home that afternoon, I had finished all my packing, done the chores, and had supper on the table.

When they all walked in the house, they were pleasantly surprised. They had expected to come home and warm up some of the leftovers from the last two days. I made Mom and Dad's favorite meal of chicken and veggie fried rice with egg rolls. The table was set with the nice tableware, and I had dimmed the lights then lit the candles just as they were walking up the walkway.

Everyone seemed to be very relaxed just as I was hoping on my last night here.

It was a little more difficult to get to sleep that night with the realization of what tomorrow would hold. I rolled over to see the clock by my bed read 2:00 a.m. That was the last thing I remembered before finally drifting off to sleep.

Sunday, April 1

I woke up at nine thirty after a restless night. I almost overslept, and at seeing how we were supposed to be at the church by ten fifteen to load our things, I rushed around and pulled on my nice blue jeans, a sweatshirt, and my leather jacket. I knew that the cool spring air would cut right through my clothes, so I put on my riding coveralls as well then pulled on my boots and was ready to split.

Mom and Dad were so wrapped up in their new life that it seemed I had all but disappeared, so today I would disappear. I slipped my journal in my backpack and headed to the barn to get my dirt bike, but as I reached for the doorknob I heard Dad's voice.

"Megan, don't you think you should tell us goodbye before you leave for church?"

"I'm running late, Dad."

To which he started his "Don't you think you owe us…" speech. After the first few words, my mind took a detour and I managed to ignore the remainder, of which I had memorized anyway.

I didn't want to hear it, so I turned, and after setting my things on the kitchen table, gave him a big hug and a smile of mortar. Then I hurried off to tell Mom and Grace good bye. For Mom, it was more of a good riddance. There was a pent-up anger boiling deep inside of me for what she had done. How could she, for all these years allow me to believe that I was their child then turn on me as if I were an old worn-out toy to be recycled? I couldn't forget to say goodbye to Aunt Kathy, so I hurried to her room and gave her a big hug, told her that I loved her, and thanked her again for the new boots. I told her I would love to spend more time saying goodbye but that I was running late, so with that I turned and walked out the bedroom door. My eyes were beginning to get misty, so I wiped the tears on my sleeve as I walked down stairs. I grabbed my bag off the table where I had left it, threw it over my shoulder, and walked out the back door.

I made it to the barn, strapped my things to the dirt bike, pulled my helmet on, and slid my leg over the cycle to straddle it. Pausing, I took one last look around then closed my eyes and thought of all of the good times I had had in that old barn. I took a slow deep breath and listened. I would never forget the sounds and smells that reminded me of what used to be.

I got to the end of our long driveway, out of sight of the house, stopped, and pulled my cell phone out to call my friend. I told her that my parents decided to keep me home to help out around the house. I made up some story about the maid being sick and that Aunt Kathy would be busy this week so they needed me to stay home. Thank goodness she bought the story and didn't ask a whole lot of questions. She said she was sorry, she would miss me, and that she would relay the message to the youth leader. I thanked her, slipped my phone back in my pocket, and headed down the road. I knew that the youth group was going to have a devotional that morning and they would try to get on the road by 11:00 a.m.

I headed down Highway 93, which is a very narrow, curvy, two-lane road. You rarely see a patrolman on this stretch and it is paved, so I figured it would be better than back roads. I planned to make it to the roadside hotel on Highway 60 in Canonsburg, Kentucky, and stay the night there. The next morning, I could stop and pick up some supplies to take to the cabin.

I did a lot of thinking while I was going down the road. I hated lying to my friend and wondered if one day we would see each other again. She was like a sister to me, and she often begged me to come to church with her. In the last few months, I went just to get out of the house. I didn't really understand the sermons and Bible readings and that sort of thing, but I did have a sense that there may be something to this relationship with the Lord stuff they talked about. I remembered that we had an old Bible on the mantle in the cabin. I think it was put there mostly for decoration or something, but maybe I'll check it out when I get there.

I took it slow, stopping several times along the road to check the time and just think. It wasn't very far to the hotel, but it was windy and the air was cool. The face shield on my helmet fogged over a couple of times which made it hard to see and somewhat dangerous to continue. My goal was to get to my first stop because I needed to pull my dirt bike into the hotel room so it would be out of sight. You see the church bus was headed in the exact same direction, and I couldn't take the chance of my friend spotting my bike.

I finally made it to the hotel and, using a fake ID, managed to get a room. It was at the far end of a long row of rooms which was perfect. Just as soon as I got my bike inside, I pulled my boots and coveralls off then threw my tired body across the bed to take a nap. I was so tired from riding on that dirt bike that I was thankful for the rest and didn't wake up until almost dark.

I wakened suddenly and had to get my wits about me and remember where I was. I looked in the mirror while washing my face and I noticed the dark circles under my eyes from not being able to sleep the last few weeks. I pulled my long dark curly hair up in a bun on the top of my head. Pulling my hair up made me look so different and much older. Feeling the hunger pangs from not eating all day, I grabbed some cash pulled on my leather jacket and went to the hotel restaurant.

I saw some people at the restaurant who I had met one time when I was visiting my friends in the Clear Creek area of Kentucky. I couldn't remember her name but they approached me, introduced themselves, and tried to get me to join them, but I was so afraid the girl would recognize me that I had to leave. I remembered that this girl had asked about the scar on my jaw when I visited with my friends in Kentucky, so I turned my head hoping that she wouldn't notice it. The memory behind the scar was so painful that I would much like to forget about it and Lord knows that I didn't need to have some one spot me and take me back to the mess I came from. I noticed the girl dropped something while at my booth but I didn't want to interact with them, so I picked it up, flipped it over, and saw that it was a baby picture. I just gave it to the cashier on my way out and pointed to the table where this family sat and said, "I believe someone from that group dropped this."

I rushed out of the restaurant, hurried to my room, and locked the door behind me. With the lingering feeling of exhaustion from the events of the day, I decided to go back to bed. I slept in my clothes so that I could leave in a hurry if necessary. I set my alarm for 5:00 a.m. and tried to get some more rest.

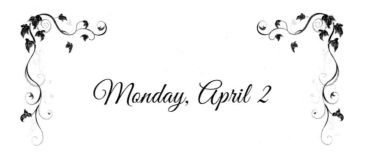

Monday, April 2

I woke at the sound of the alarm, but when I turned, I noticed that it was only 4:30 a.m. I jumped out of bed, walked to the window, and slightly moved the curtain to look outside. I noticed there were cops, fire trucks, and a couple of ambulances out front. Panic seized me and I just about turned the light on to collect my things and leave. I stopped short of the switch and remembered that people on the outside would notice and I didn't want to draw any unwanted attention.

After my eyes adjusted to the darkness, I slipped my jacket on then pulled my coveralls up, hooking the straps, and finally slid my boots on. I strapped my things back onto my cycle and slipped my wallet in my pocket. I took another look outside to try to make out what was going on. It appeared that the fuel station next door had a car that was on fire and there was a threat of an explosion. I also noticed that other people had been stirred awake from all the commotion. There was an officer who was assisting the hotel manager in going from room to room in an effort to evacuate the hotel due to the danger of an explosion.

They were still at the other end of the row of rooms, so I opened the door and rolled my cycle out and around the corner, hoping not to be noticed. There was a utility shed setting about a hundred feet away with nothing but the dark of night between, so I pushed my cycle to the shed and watched from there as people were being told to evacuate. I saw a crowd of panic-stricken people in a hurry to get far away from the danger that seemed imminent. Then I noticed the family who had asked me to join them at the restaurant last night loading things into their vehicle. I was glad they were safe, but I couldn't afford to encounter them again for fear the girl would recognize me.

I watched as they rushed to get their things, and when they left, they drove in the direction from which I had come.

I stood behind the shed nearly an hour and a half, waiting for the sun to come up and watching as the hotel cleared of its occupants. At the break of dawn, I straddled my cycle, got it started, and headed for the cabin and my new life.

I decided on backtracking to Huntington, West Virginia, to pick up supplies. Although in the past we had stopped here to shop, I knew that it was a place where people were not so familiar with my family, and therefore, I wasn't as likely to be recognized. I got a few canned meats, some jerky, a loaf of bread, and some snacks—mostly things that didn't have to be cooked or heated for eating. This would keep me from using electricity.

I thought I had better pick up another phone—one of those prepaid phones—so I couldn't be traced. When I walked out the door of the big shopping center, I dropped my phone into the trash, only after taking the battery out of it. I went down the road a ways and stopped to get some fuel and throw the battery in their trash can by the pumps.

I took off from the gas station and it wasn't long before I finally arrived at the cabin. I pulled up close to the cabin to unload my belongings then parked the cycle in the shed out back. It was getting to be late afternoon, and with this being early spring, I felt the damp cool air move in.

I decided to start a fire in the fireplace to knock off the chill. I noticed on the mantle above the fireplace the decorative box that contained the family Bible. I set aside the thought of taking it down to look through it until after I finished putting things away and getting something ready to eat for it was well after lunch and my stomach didn't hesitate telling me it was time to eat.

After I finished eating, I took down the box, blew the dust from the top, which nearly choked me, and headed to the table ready to explore the Bible for words of wisdom. I noticed that this box was rather heavy for its size. I was surprised, as I opened the box, to find not a Bible but a fireproof lockbox. I pulled the lockbox out and immediately wondered where they had hid the key, so I left the box on the table and began to search for the key.

I walked into the bathroom and had a strange memory of Mom standing on her tiptoes, reaching the top of the medicine cabinet. I had startled her when I stood in the doorway and asked her what she was doing. I must have been five or six years old, but I remember her telling me she was searching for dust bunnies and told me that I should go look for these bunnies in my room until she found hers and then she would come get me and we would play another game.

I stretched to reach the top of the cabinet then decided it would be easier to stand on the toilet and step over on to the sink. Using the tips of my fingers, as if reading Braille, I felt the top of the medicine cabinet. I was moving my fingers fast enough that when I reached the key, the key went flying off the cabinet landing somewhere below. I jumped off the sink to the floor searching for my treasured key. After finding it, I ran to the kitchen table to take a look inside the mysterious box.

Inside I found some papers bundled together with rubber bands. Most of the bands broke as I was taking them off, but that didn't surprise me. From the looks of them they had been on there for a very long time. They had that dry crackled look like some old cowboy who had ridden the dusty trail way too long. I unfolded the papers, and to my surprise, they were my adoption papers. It had the name of the law firm who handled the adoption and the name of my birth mom.

They had gone all the way to New York to adopt me. I wondered why they had done that when there were numerous agencies and lawyers in the state of Ohio who would be glad to find a child for a wealthy doctor and his wife. I remember seeing pictures of Mom when she was supposedly pregnant with me. My head started spinning with confusion and I had to stop to take a deep breath.

After reading the adoption papers, I looked in the bottom of the box and found some newspaper clippings. They had a picture of a man in handcuffs being led away by police. Under the picture, I read the caption "Terrance

Hubb, well known New York lawyer, arrested for illegal adoptions and associations with a human trafficking ring."

The article went on to tell of his activities in snatching and selling babies. The people who adopted the babies were simply charged outrageous adoption fees while keeping them in the dark as to the truth of how these children were obtained.

The words of the paper started to blur and I had to dry the tears from my eyes to continue reading. Tears continued, causing several stains on the paper by the time I had finished the article. I was beginning to believe the lady whose name appeared on the adoption papers as my birth mother was in fact no blood kin to me but a stranger as well.

I had lived most of my life rather sure of who I was and what I wanted to do with my life when I grew up. Now here I was three years from becoming an adult and feeling like I needed to go back and learn to walk all over again. I needed time to figure out who I really was, where my biological parents were, did they really give me up, or was I one of those who had been kidnapped? If the latter, did my parents even know that I'm alive or had they exhausted all possibilities and hope, believing me to have perished? With all these thoughts whirling around in my mind, I began to wonder if I had siblings or if I was an only child.

I went to put the news article along with the adoption papers back into the lock box. I noticed yet another paper in the bottom of this box. When I pulled it out and unfolded it, there before my eyes was a poster. It was one of those Missing posters, and on it was a picture of a baby. A baby girl named Bella. Bella Longhenry.

Next to the baby picture was one of those age-enhanced pictures which had aged her up to nine years old. At least I know that this family hadn't given up searching for their daughter even eight years after she had disappeared. I then realized that the people who I thought were my parents not only adopted me but later suspected that I had been abducted as an infant and adopted illegally. Yet they chose to keep me, allowing this poor family to believe I was gone forever, possibly even dead.

Through my mind went a flash of the picture I handed the cashier at the restaurant. I looked again at the picture of the baby on the missing poster. I dropped the paper and ran to the toilet to throw up what I had eaten earlier. I screamed and cried, spewing obscenities from my mouth, my words filled with anger, disbelief and, yes, hatred, until I had exhausted every ounce of energy in my body. I managed to make it to the bed and didn't remember anything until I woke up the next morning.

Tuesday, April 3

My head pounded as the light of dawn bore through the gap in the curtains, making it hard to sleep any longer. It was dreadfully difficult to open my eyes as they were swollen from crying the night before. I also suffered pain and stiffness throughout my body from my intense emotional breakdown, after I realized what these people, who called themselves my parents all these years, had done, not only to me but to my biological parents as well.

I went to the medicine cabinet to search for something for my headache. After swallowing a pain reliever, I walked to the kitchen and ate a few bites of a donut. I wasn't really hungry, but I knew I needed something in my stomach after taking that medicine. I decided that I was going to try to find out who my real parents were, and if possible, locate them. I just didn't know for sure where to start.

I went back to the adoption papers. I figured that would be a good place as any to start. There were surely names and phone numbers or something that would be of use in finding them. Then I remembered the poster of the missing child. I slowly pulled it out and there listed below the pictures were several phone numbers, one being the number of the Mr. and Mrs. Phillips. I reached for my cell phone and slowly punched in the numbers.

The phone rang a couple of times then there was a funny noise and it sounded like the call had been forwarded. Then an answering machine clicked on, but I lost my nerve and hung up. My mind was full of so many questions like: What if these aren't my parents? What was the funny noise on the line? Why didn't I listen to the message before hanging up?

I had answered the last question in my mind. I simply didn't want to talk to a machine; I needed to speak to a real live human. I took another look at the poster and decided to call the next number on the list. I kept practicing, in my head, what I would say to the person who answered the call. As I was thinking, a lady's voice came on the line.

"Hello. This is Nancy Andrews. How may I help you?"

I cleared my throat as it seemed to tighten all of a sudden, and the tears began to flow.

"I think I may be the girl on a "Missing" poster and I don't know…I just…I…um…I…I…"

My mind was so full, and it seemed all my emotions were spent. I just sat in silence for what felt like an eternity. Then I heard Nancy's voice. She had such a kind tender voice. It was warm and made me feel so comfortable.

"Can you tell me your name, honey?"

"Megan—well, that's what I've been called for nearly fifteen years."

"Megan, can you tell me the name of the girl whose picture is on the poster?"

"Bella" I said as my voice quivered. "Bella Longhenry."

I thought the connection had been dropped as there was a long period of nothingness. Then I thought I could hear a sniffle from the lady on the other end.

"Megan, can you tell me where you live?"

"I…well…I don't know. I will tell you that I used to live in Oak Hill, Ohio. But… well…I just don't know…I really don't have a home anymore."

"Are you safe? Is anyone hurting you, Megan?"

"I have shelter. I really think I need to go. I'm tired and I need some time to think. Would it be okay if I call you later?"

"Yes, yes, that would be fine. May I pray with you before you go?"

"I guess that would be okay."

Nancy prayed and ended by asking the Lord to watch over and protect me. When she said "In Jesus, Amen," I had this sense that someone or something indeed had been and would continue to watch over me.

There was a warm, calming peaceful feeling that came over me that I had never felt before in my life. I wondered what it could be, then I remembered one of the pastor's sermons about how the love of the Jesus would give us a deep abiding peace. Maybe he does exist after all.

I went out to haul some wood into the cabin. Then, leaving the mess on the table, I took a walk to try to clear my head. I wandered down an old, rugged but familiar trail I had taken many a time when we came here as a family. Some favorite spots I always loved to visit were the rocky bluffs where I stopped to think. One could look out over the valley and across to the opposite slope filled with trees of various kinds, and as you continued down the trail, you came upon a spring that bubbled fresh water up from the earth. Down in the valley, there was a place where the spring waters pooled before flowing over the flat rocks where it dropped three feet, creating a miniature waterfall. This was the spot where I usually pulled my shoes and socks off to dip my feet in the cool water, but it was downright cold this time of year and I shivered at the thought of doing that today. After meandering through the woods, I turned to head back to the cabin, feeling somewhat invigorated and ready to tell Nancy all that was on my heart and mind.

Upon approach, I spotted someone coming down the road in an old, beat-up Chevy van. The springs squeaked as it went down the rocky rutted road and the thing rattled so loud that it was no secret they were coming. As they were nearing the cabin, I noticed the passenger tipping a dark brown bottle to his lips and trying to sing to the seventies music they had cranked up loud. I crouched down behind some thick brush, which was on the side of the road down from the cabin, hoping they wouldn't see me. I could feel my pulse throughout my body, and as panic welled up inside, I tried to take slow deep breaths in an effort to remain clam. The vehicle slowed and I thought it was going to stop, but just about then a puff of smoke rolled out of the chimney and they drove on down the rugged road towards where I was. I got a good look at them as they drove past where I had taken cover. The passenger chucked his empty bottle out the window, nearly hitting me in the head. They didn't appear to be well kempt, in fact they looked down right creepy with long matted hair and the odor was enough to make me puke. I stayed in the cover until I couldn't hear the vehicle then I made a beeline for the cabin.

I knew the road going by our house came to a dead end four miles ahead, where the Crawford cabin sat. I wondered if they had intentions of seeking a place to sleep or if they were thieves. The thoughts of them possibly returning to cause trouble put such a fear in me that I began to wonder if I should pack up and leave. Then I recalled the phone call I made earlier and decided that I would grab the phone and call this Nancy lady. I dialed and the phone was busy. I hung up and waited for a few seconds and dialed again, still busy. I dialed repeatedly in hopes that it would ring through. I felt somewhat panicked then I remembered that there were other phone numbers on that poster back in the house.

I hurried back to the house and grabbed the poster then I got my things put together and hauled them out to the shed. There wasn't much wood in the fireplace, so I didn't bother putting the fire out. I know that I had been taught differently but I wasn't sure that I would even be leaving at this point.

I hurried back to the shed and sat there on an old log bench just inside the door and pulled out the poster. I thought I heard the van coming back this way and I dropped the paper. I was so shook that I couldn't hold onto the paper, so with trembling hands I hit the redial on the phone, deciding to try Nancy's number one more time.

I started to sob thinking that she may never answer and I would be all alone to deal with what may be headed my way. My thoughts were scrambled then I heard the soft kind voice from before.

"Hello? Hello? Is anybody there?"

My throat tightened and my voice shook so bad that I didn't even recognize myself when I finally got the words to come out of my mouth. "I think I may be in danger" was all I managed to get out.

"Megan, can you tell me your location? I want to try to get some people out there to help you."

"I'm on the northwest finger of the lake and in a remote area called Gilbert Lane. I'm scared. Can you tell them to hurry, please?" These were the last words I spoke before the deafening silence and the realization of the connection being lost.

I felt vulnerable like a small wounded critter with vultures circling over head just waiting for the right time to have their fill. I stuck my hand inside my pants pocket to get the keys to my cycle, but as I reached the bottom of the pocket, I could feel nothing but small pieces of lint. I quickly reached into the other pocket with the same result. I couldn't believe it; I swore I picked the keys up off the table and put them in my pocket this morning before I left for my walk. I retraced my tracks in my mind and realized that I could have possibly lost them on the trail or maybe they were still lying on the table inside the cabin.

I ran to the back of the cabin, on the north side, where I knew nobody would be able to see me from the road. I slipped around the to the west end, where Mom and Dad's bedroom was, and peeked around the corner to see if I could get a look at who may be coming up the road. My worst fears had come true. The old beat-up van was headed this way. I knew I needed to get inside the cabin to check for the keys before they got much closer. I opened the bedroom window and crawled inside hitting the floor with a thud. I jumped to my feet and ran to the table fast as I could but there were no keys. I could hear the van slow and come to a stop. I reached the front door and locked it just as I heard someone step onto the wooden walkway leading to the front door. I turned to go to the bedroom with the intentions of slipping back out the same way I entered, but I caught a glimpse of a long-haired man walking past the kitchen window. I hurried to the bedroom to close the window I had left open. I got it shut and lay beneath it with my back hugging the wall, in hopes that if he looked in, he wouldn't see me.

I felt my heart pounding while the rest of my body was frozen with fear. I closed my eyes and cried out to this God of whom my friend Sandy, her preacher Kenny, and Nancy had all spoken of. "God, please God if you are really there, please Help me."

I heard someone knock on the front door and shake the door knob. Then the man at the front hollered, "Hey Daryl, come here, I think you can easily pick this lock."

Daryl was standing right by the window I had closed a few seconds earlier when he answered with, "Are you sure that nobody is home?"

I closed my eyes and prayed that he would go around to the front so that I could slip out the window. While I was lying there on the floor, I suddenly remembered where the lost keys were. I had left them on the bathroom sink. I heard the crunching of old, dead, dried-up leaves as Daryl moved slowly away from the window. The sound of his footsteps would stop every so often and it dawned on me that he could be trying to look through the windows.

I knew I had to make a go for it. I did a belly crawl to the doorway, stood up then looked in every direction

I thought they could possibly see me from a window. I slipped out into the short hall and across to the bathroom. Quickly I reached for the keys but knocked them off the sink instead. At that moment, something funny happened. There was a gust of wind that suddenly picked up then died down just as quickly.

I heard Daryl holler, "Did you hear something?"

It sounded like he was almost to the front of the cabin when he spoke, so I froze in place for a bit, afraid to move.

The other man laughed and said, "Daryl, I think you've had way too much to drink. Why, they ain't no sound but these wind chimes a chimin' in the breeze."

I remember hating that Mom put those chimes up. They were real annoying when I tried to get to sleep and the wind would be causing those things to clank. Right at this moment though, I was very thankful for them and all the noise they made.

Could this be God, answering my prayer for help? Could it be that he cares for me even though I barely know him?

I didn't have time to get these questions answered right this minute. I picked the keys off the floor just as another gust of wind came up. I slipped them in my pocket and headed for the bedroom window. I could hear the front door knob being jiggled as these potential intruders attempted to work their way in. I slipped the window up and crawled out. I didn't have time to try to close it. I just headed to the shed as quick as my feet would carry me.

I had reached the door of the shed when I heard Daryl holler, "Hey you pretty little thing, wha' cha leavin' for?"

Chills ran up my spine as I reached my bike. Not having time to put my helmet on, I straddled the bike, put the key in the on position, and started kicking the starter. It took several times kicking the thing before I heard it turn over. I put it in gear, gave it gas, and let out on the clutch. It popped a wheelie, and I almost hit Daryl as I left the shed.

Daryl spun around and tried to grab me but missed. The other man came running toward me, and I left the pathway and went on to even rougher ground. I managed to make it to the road and decided that I was in more trouble than I could handle. Even if it meant having to go back to the Felt household, I needed help. Going as fast as I possibly could, I headed for the park ranger's station.

I could hear that old van start up and knew that these two were not giving up very easily, but I had an advantage as long as I kept my head about me. The road was very narrow and rough. They wouldn't be able to travel as fast as I could on my cycle. With the small bike, it was easier especially since I knew the layout of the land and almost had the rough spots memorized from the frequent visits we made to our little bit of heaven. It was the norm that we loaded my bike in the truck when we came to the cabin and I dearly loved to ride around these country trails.

I had a change of mind about going to the ranger station; instead, I took a shortcut where I knew the van wouldn't be able to go. It was rough going but it got me to the road that led to the Brooks' home. Although most people had cabins in these parts as a summer get away, the Brooks had built a large cabin and made it their permanent home. They were friendly people and I often babysat for them when we came to Grayson. They were people I trusted and this was a lot closer than the ranger station anyway.

I cut across the rough terrain and into a wooded area. I thought I was making good time, but looking over my shoulder, I noticed that the van wasn't too far behind. I swerved more than once to miss some branches along the small trail, but this time I hit a rut that had been camouflaged by the grass that had grown over it. I struggled as the front end of the bike wobbled a bit, but I was able to get it back under control. That was when I heard the bullet whiz through the air and ping the tail of the bike.

Tears started to stream down my face from fear as well as the wind and my hair whipping me in the eyes. This may well be my last ride and I had no one to tell good bye. Thoughts went reeling through my mind of who my real parents might be and if I had any brothers or sisters. Had they long ago given up hope of ever finding me? I would like to think not. There was a strong desire and determination that surged through my body to make it through this alive, so I opened the throttle on the cycle and rode as if fire were at my heels.

At one point, I thought I heard someone calling my name but while riding at this speed, I needed to stay focused on the path ahead. I decided to believe it was my imagination just blowing past my ears in the wind. The only hope I had now was to make it to the Brooks' cabin, and at this point in time, even that seemed hopeless. I hadn't wanted to get them involved for fear one of them or their children being harmed or even killed.

Time seemed to stand still and everything was running like the slow motion replay they show in the football games on TV. My heart pounded so hard that I knew my chest would explode if this wild ride didn't end soon.

I had so many things running through my mind that it was hard to even say a meaningful prayer. Somehow, though, I could feel that someone or something was there protecting me through all of this.

I looked up and saw the Brooks' cabin, and suddenly I felt a calm peace come over my whole body. As I approached the cabin, Mr. Brooks stepped out on his porch and waved his hand, pointing to the rear of the cabin. I noticed in his other hand was his rifle which he held close to his side and pointing down. I veered off the road and took the small path that lead to their back door. As I came close to the back door I saw it was being held open by Mrs. Abby Brooks. I spun my bike to a swift stop and leaped off it at a dead run through the back door. I heard the door slam and lock behind me then Mrs. Brooks grabbed me by the arm and headed me to their cellar along with their children.

She slammed the cellar door shut and locked it as well then took a brief moment to hug me tight. She reached above the door where they had a spare rifle and she cocked it. Then she turned to me and told me to grab the spare ammo from the top shelf to the right of the door. As I reached for the ammo, I heard a gun blast and I lost my nerve. My body began to tremble then I felt a hand on my shoulder and heard the voice of Mrs. Brooks.

"I really need you to keep it together now. We all have to think straight to get through this."

She continued. "I need you to take the children through the passageway to the barn. You will come to a small room there under the tack room. I need you to stay there with the doors locked till someone comes for you."

She then moved the shelves, opened the door behind them, and handed me their youngest child as we entered the tunnel. She hurried us along, and I could hear her close the door behind us then move the shelves back in place.

There was an eerie silence as we made our way to the shelter in the barn. I felt a twinge of pain in the calf of my leg. I figured that I must have pulled something when I leaped off my bike, but I didn't have time to think of such things at the time, so I focused on getting the children to the safe room. The children were frightened because they knew using this passageway meant that there was trouble. They had been taught by their parents that this was for their safety. I was trying to comfort the children when we heard the gunfire continue.

As I was stumbling through a prayer, Lizzie, the eldest daughter, joined in. "Abba, Yahweh, please keep Mom and Dad safe. I pray for the safety of all the good people who are trying to help. Keep us in Your loving hands. In the name of Yeshua, Your Son. Amen!"

I was amazed at the prayer. I had never heard of Abba, Yahweh, or Yeshua before and wondered who she could be praying to. I also noticed that, at such a young age, she prayed with sincerity and authority like she knew these people well enough that her requests would be heard and answered.

As a matter of fact, the minute she said "Amen," the gunfire ceased. I began to look at Lizzie with my head tilted and an expression that must have shown my disbelief in what had just taken place.

Lizzie just looked at me with a big beautiful smile of confidence and said, "He always listens."

I remembered one of the many visits with this family. They had tried to share their beliefs with us, but the conversation was abruptly changed by Doc. They shared that God had in fact told them the names they were to give each of their children. After the birth of each child, they would pray and ask God, "Who is this child?" Lizzie was short for Elizabeth but they said that her name was taken from the Bible. Its origin was Hebrew and meant "oath of God." The spiritual connotation was "consecrated."

Elizabeth was their first child. They had tried for many years to have children. Both Mr. and Mrs. Brooks believed that God would answer their prayers, so while they prayed what to name their firstborn, it seemed very fitting that she was to be named "oath of God" and thus they consecrated her to him.

I always remembered this because I thought that it was very special that parents would take such extreme care in even naming a child.

The sound of sirens broke through my flow of thoughts. The pounding at the door made me jump with fear then I heard Mr. Brooks' voice and my fears melted away. There were other voices out there, but none that I recognized until I heard someone address Pastor Deter. I instantly remembered the man and girl who had approached me at the hotel restaurant. As the door opened and we were helped out, the children ran to their parents, and I handed the baby to Mrs. Brooks. She hugged me and with tears streaming down her cheeks, she whispered, "Thank God you are all safe."

I was somewhat relieved as I scanned the myriad of people and realized that my adoptive parents were not here. There were policemen with their K9s, an ambulance, and what looked to be a news crew setting up cameras. My eyes caught sight of the pastor and Kylie along with Mrs. Deter and Jeff. Kylie and I gazed at each other for some time before we both started weeping and walking toward one another. I knew there was something that seemed so familiar about her, but I couldn't put my finger on what it was. I just knew that there was a strange sort of connection between us.

Just as we embraced there was the sound of another vehicle approaching the house. Fearing that it was Mom and Dad coming for me, I stepped back, almost pushing Kylie away. I carefully watched as people exited the vehicle and started to approach. Kylie turned to see who I was gazing at then she took her brother by the arm and headed toward these people. I had no clue as to who they were, so I drew close to the Brooks family whom I felt safest with for now.

Together At Last

Strangers

Kylie turned to look in the direction of my gaze then she and Jeff took off running toward the strangers. I watched as a man and woman both grabbed Kylie and Jeff and held them. I could hear the wailing cries coming from the four and wondered what could possibly be so distressing for all of them to be making such noises. They embraced for what seemed an eternity then Kylie turned and pointed in my direction.

I tried to stay out of sight of the news media who were being cordoned off behind yellow crime scene tape, yet I kept my eye on the group of people heading in my direction. They all had a glow about them and smiles on their radiant faces that spoke loudly of love. I felt strangely warm and drawn to them. I was reminded of that reoccurring dream that I had been having and wondered if it had anything to do with what was taking place at this moment.

Suddenly, I could smell a hint of sulfur in the air as my senses became heightened. I heard the dogs in the distance as they ran through the woods on the trail of one of the perpetrators. There were officers and rescue workers shouting above the noise of the helicopter that was overhead. My heart began pounding and the closer this group of people got to me, the harder it seemed to pound. As I held my breath, it felt very much like the world was closing in on me. Things started to fade, and I faintly remembered the pain in my leg.

As things grew dim, I thought, *Is this what it feels like when someone dies?*

My legs turned to rubber, causing me to feel that I was way too heavy for them. The weakness was overtaking me. *Numbness...What...what...what is this numbness, try breathing...yes, breath deep, keep your eyes open, focus. Nothing is working, I just can't fight it. Where am I? What is happening? Darkness I can't see... I hear voices but I can't see. What's happening?*

I hear Elizabeth's voice and she is once again talking to the same people she prayed to in the shelter. I hear her praying for healing... now there are other voices drowning hers out.

I can hear people calling for Bella. Who is Bella? Why doesn't she answer? Someone is crying for her now...Wait, now they are calling for Megan. That's me, I...I think. I just can't answer. I feel so tired I think I will sleep now. I said I am tired. Leave me alone, please, *stop yelling. What are you doing? Ouch, what just bit me? Get it off me. I can't move. Please get it off me. Didn't you hear me? Something just bit me and I am so tired I can't move. Now would you please get it off me? What is going on? What do you mean, "Okay, on the count of three?" What's happening? Can anybody hear me?! What is this? I feel like I am floating. There is wind and a* whoow whoow *sound, people keep yelling, "Keep pressure on it." And nobody will answer any of my requests. Oh this constant motion. I think I am going to throw up. Can someone please stop this Ferris wheel? I need to get off before*

I get sick. What good does any of this do? This is like talking to the wind. I think I must be dreaming. If I just go back to sleep, and when I wake up in the morning everything will be alright. I will be back in my own bed...Wait a minute I left home and...and...I keep hearing people call my name. They keep asking me all these questions that I can't answer. I just can't seem to get my vocal cords to comply. I feel like I am moving around on this cloud. My eyes, I can't seem to open them since everything went dark, so I will sleep now.

Kylie:
My Secret Place

As we were walking toward Bella, Jeff holding Dad's hand and Mom holding mine, we noticed that Bella turned pale. Her eyes widened and she dropped to the ground. A group of people were around her, and Abby Brooks knelt beside her with her oldest daughter.

Dad turned and called out to one of the paramedics. He had noticed that Bella's pant leg looked wet and the jeans had a tear in them. We all knew that she had a hail of bullets coming at her as she rode her motorcycle to the Brooks' cabin, but until now we had believed she was fine.

All four of us ran toward her, and there was such a commotion that Abby took her children into the house so they wouldn't be in the way. I looked up to see her oldest daughter looking out the window. Her lips were moving, and by the look on her face I believe she was praying.

I began praying as well. "Oh Dear God, my sister! God, please, we haven't even gotten to tell her that she is our sister. Please don't let her die."

Two rather muscular men were carrying a stretcher as others ran ahead of them to check on Bella. One of the paramedics asked what her name was and my parents both said, "Bella." The medics started calling out to her to get her to respond. That is when Mr. Brooks stepped in and said, "Her name is Megan."

My parents stepped back and let them work on her without any interruptions. They knew that if she were to respond, it would be to the name she had grown up with. In fact we all stood back and prayed, asking God to bring her back to us once again. Once they got her onto the stretcher and headed to the helicopter, the cops had us all go into the cabin, for safety reasons, while the chopper was taking off. We watched out the window as they took her away. Dad asked a policeman where they were taking her, and they told him that only family could be informed of the location. Walt stepped up and showed them a paper, and they gave Dad the information. While all this was happening, Mr. Brooks was on the phone with Doc Felt.

When he got off the phone, Walt sat down with Mr. Brooks and showed him a picture of Bella when she was a baby. Mr. Brooks confirmed that this was the baby picture of the now teenage girl he knew as Megan. Walt shared the story of how the baby had been kidnapped and adopted out by an illegal agency. Both Mr. and Mrs. Brooks wept as they heard the story. They had known the Felt family for nearly twenty years and all this was a shock to them.

We realized that the Brooks family had a strong tie with this girl whom they had always known as Megan, and this was just as hard on them as anyone else who knew her. Everyone involved would have healing to work through and even though this was just the beginning, it would be postponed for yet more time. We did go with Mr. Brooks to the Felt cabin to check things out before going to the hospital. When he opened the door, we found a box along with a mess of papers lying on the table. As Dad drew closer to the table, he noticed the Missing poster of Bella when she was a baby. He sobbed as he picked it up along with the other papers and held them close to his heart. Dad noticed the newspaper clipping of the lawyer who was arrested for selling babies, and it matched the name on the adoption papers. We could that see he was deeply moved and we were all quiet, watching as he and Mom hugged. They then drew us between the two of them and held us tight. This was when they realized that Megan had found out that she had been kidnapped and adopted out.

We all knew that the days ahead would determine whether or not Bella would make it through her injuries, and so we all decided to focus on her for now and deal with the rest of the mess when she was well enough to handle it. This time would give Mom, Dad, Jeff, and I the chance to do some of our own healing as well. Even though we now realized that we had an older sister and there was a bit of excitement about it all, it may take Jeff and me quite some time to adjust to all that had happened.

During a quiet time, I couldn't help but notice what mom had written in her journal. I could relate to this quite well as mom taught us to do this from a young age. She told us that writing a journal helps to learn and heal. By putting our thoughts and events of the day down, you can see where you could do things differently or see where you have grown through an experience. One can tell of the joys and pleasures of life too. Mom was one who loved to write poetry and was able to express herself through the words she put on paper. Later, she would share a poem that she had written:

Here in My Secret Place

I started this journey with you
Here in my secret place
Not knowing a thing about you
I only imagined seeing you face to face

The day I found that you existed
Was filled with great joy
Not even having knowledge yet
If you were to be a girl or a boy

As the days turned into weeks
And months would seem more like years
The day came when you were born
It was filled great excitement and tears

Then came that fateful day
Filled with our greatest mourning
When some one snatched you away
And you were gone from us without warning

There was later a wonderful surprise
But before anyone knew
I had two more who were here
In my same secret place as you

We never, ever gave up hope
Of finding you alive
Praying each day for safety
And that we all would survive

To make it this far
Only to lose you again, my dear
Would be too much to bear
Way too much for all, I fear

So we will all join in prayer
Asking our Heavenly Father
To heal you completely
As our friend, sister and daughter

With love,
Mom

Walt drove us to the hospital as the pastor and Adel followed in their vehicle.

When we arrived, we all took a seat and Dad went to the clerk to ask about Megan's condition. Just then Doc Felt walked in and heard Dad talking with the clerk. His eyes widened as he approached the clerk and asked about Megan as well. The clerk asked if we were all family and Doc said, "Not that I am aware of."

Walt, Dad, and Mom asked Doc if they could sit down and talk with him. He asked, "Do I have a choice?"

To which Walt replied, "Most everybody here has a choice, but there are some in this world who haven't."

With this, Doc agreed to talk with them. They went to the private family room that was located in the corner of the large waiting room while we were left with Pastor and Adel. Just before entering the room, Doc paused, then turned and gazed at me with a look of disbelief, as if he were reminded of Megan. I hadn't thought of it much until then, but we did resemble each other quite a lot. I think that was the defining moment when he realized what was happening and maybe sensed that we were Megan's family.

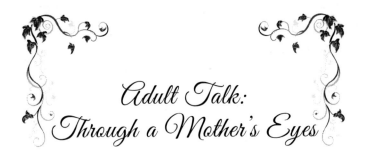

Adult Talk:
Through a Mother's Eyes

After Mr. Felt, Walt, Sam, and I entered the small room, we all took a seat and Walt started the conversation.

"This situation we all find ourselves in today is one of great pain for all concerned. First off, we all have a deep connection to this young lady who is now in the face of death and this alone is so troubling to each one here. Dr. Felt, I am Walt." Then pointing to us, he said, "And this is Sam and Ann Longhenry."

"We all want you to know that we are first and foremost here because of our concern for Megan. At this moment in time, we are focused on her recovery. We don't want to do anything that will hinder this. We understand that this situation must be hard on you and your wife as well and we will respect you through this."

Doc hung his head and had tears streaming down his cheeks. He then looked up and said, "Thank you. This is a very difficult time. My wife just gave birth to our daughter and now this. We thought that Megan was away at church camp. We believed she was safe and didn't even know that she had run away or why she would do such a thing."

Something strange happened. It was as if this man sitting before us had to relieve his mind and heart of all that he had held in. It was just like a dam, which had held all this guilt in, had burst wide open to rid him of the unseen pressures of his life.

He started out in a quivering voice telling us that Megan had been adopted because he and his wife had tried for years to have their own children without success. He continued. "When we decided to adopt, I had heard that there was an agency in New York that dealt in quick adoptions, and we were even able to describe what we wanted our baby to look like. We had both thought this was a dream come true and that it was very expensive. We didn't know, we had no idea that these children were being kidnapped then sold. We were only happy that we had our own baby. God forgive me, we had no clue. We were so blinded by being able to have a baby that there were no other concerns as to where this child came from. It wasn't until Megan was four years old that we stumbled on her baby picture from a Missing Child poster. We contacted our lawyer who ran the adoption agency and we were given the run-around. It was then that we received a threatening phone call saying that we should just drop it all and be happy that we have a baby or our baby may just find another home. We told the person on the line that we understood and there would be no further questions. We lived in fear for some years after this happened, feeling like maybe we were being watched. We decided to move to the southern part of Ohio where we tried to live a normal life. Then we read in the paper that a human trafficking ring was busted and the lawyer who handled our adoption was involved. Nobody ever tried contacting us about Megan. We lived in fear that the perpetrators would find us so we stayed low for a long time after the bust. We attempted to go on with life as normal as one could. We never let on that Megan wasn't our own child. It was difficult knowing that after all these years, we may have to tell her about being adopted, and not only that, but that she had been kidnapped. We thought, after all the time that had passed, it would just be easier to forget the fact that she had been taken from other people."

That was when Sam handed the papers that we had found in their cabin over to Mr. Felt. He looked at them and immediately recognized them. "How did you get these?"

Sam answered, "They were lying on the table in your cabin. We believe that Megan knows the truth, but she doesn't know that we are her biological parents."

Doc raised his head. There was a look of shock and shame that came over his face. Doc asked us if we were requesting a paternity test.

There was an anger that stirred inside of me, and I was about to open my unfiltered mouth when the Holy Spirit, along with my husband's arm pulling me close to his side, caused me to remain silent.

Sam then spoke up and said, "I suppose that would be the right thing to do if you need proof that we are her biological parents. Now that you have your own daughter, I think you will understand me when I tell you that we have suffered for the last fourteen years of our lives, not knowing where our daughter was, if she was alive, dead, or worse yet if she was being used in some sort of bad way. I could only pray that she was being well taken care of if she was alive. So you have no clue as to why she would want to run away? I pray for her sake and yours that she wasn't being abused."

Mr. Felt looked up squarely into Sam's eyes, saying, "She was well taken care of, sir, and you can rest assured that if anyone so much as looked at her in the wrong way, they would have had me to deal with."

The conversation ended abruptly when the OR nurse knocked at the door.

She came into the room and gave a brief update on Megan. She had made it through surgery but had lost a lot of blood. They expected a full recovery, but she needed rest. She had actually had two wounds but the leg was the worst of the two.

I noticed that Kylie and Jeff were intently looking at us from where they sat, through the large window of the room we were in. I excused myself and went to tell them the news of Megan.

Walt, Dr. Felt, and Sam walked out of the room. I took Kylie and Jeff by the hand leading them to the privacy room. Sam followed us in and we all sat down to have some more family time. We all bowed our heads to pray while Sam led the prayer. We explained to Kylie and Jeff what happened on that Friday when we went missing and that we had people watching them to make sure they were all right. We told them of the dangers of trying to contact them while we were away and that a lot of times all we could do was trust God to take care of us all.

I wanted them to understand that we were about to tell them about Bella during spring break and let them know all that we were involved in. We believed that they were old enough to be able to handle the news of Bella and the dangers surrounding our missions.

Sam and I were actually surprised at the reaction of our children. It was as if they had grown up to accept a responsibility that should not have been theirs. We knew we had God and his servants to thank for their safety and this unusual maturity we saw in them. The thing they had the hardest time dealing with was whether or not we were all right or if we would be returning home. They told us that Pastor Chuck and Adel had had many talks with them about trusting God and having a good healthy response to times of trouble. Chuck had taught them not only to pray but to listen to God and hear what he had to say. Pastor had told them, "It is two-way communication."

Just in the short time we were gone, Kylie and Jeff had grown so much spiritually, mentally, and emotionally that it brought tears to our eyes. Jeff told us how he and Kylie took turns reading aloud from my Bible and how they learned from this to earnestly seek God—not just make their requests known to him, but also to listen to the Holy Spirit's guiding.

We were amazed at how willing they were to forgive us for all that we had put them through. It reminded me of how God spoke to me about forgiving others as he had forgiven me. I realized that one is never too young or too old to learn the lesson of forgiveness.

Megan

When I woke up, I looked around and saw the IV that had been placed in my left arm. Everything seemed like a blur of a dream and I closed my eyes. I heard the door open. The nurse came in and gently touched my arm. I opened my eyes and whispered, "Kylie, can I see Kylie?

I remember she was the last person that I saw before everything went dark, and there was some way that we had a connection. My first thought was to see her and ask her some questions that, for some reason, I believed she had the answers to. The nurse told me she would see what she could do since I was only allowed one visitor at a time. After taking my vital signs, she left the room.

I felt weak as a newborn kitten, needing to be nourished after all that had happened. I tried to think back on the events of the last few days and had chills go up my spine when I realized that I could have died. I had never gotten myself into this kind of trouble before and wondered what was awaiting me when I got out of the hospital. I knew that I didn't want to go back to what I had known as home. I suddenly thought of Aunt Kathy and wondered if she had heard the news yet. I hoped that she wasn't disappointed in me for running off like I did and causing all this grief for everyone. She was always so kind, gentle, and understanding that I didn't want to cause her any pain.

The doctor came into my room and asked if I was up to having some company. He said that my dad was out in the waiting room and was asking about me. I dreaded seeing him before I was able to speak with Kylie, so as awful and cold as it sounded, I insisted on talking with Kylie first. He said that he would have to discuss that with my dad and then he would send one of them in. He turned to leave and the door shut behind him.

I took a deep breath then exhaled. "Please, God, let it be Kylie who comes through the door. Please."

At the Request of My Sister

The doctor came into the waiting room where we were all gathered awaiting further updates on Megan. He pulled Mr. Felt to the side and talked to him in a low soft voice. Dr. Felt slowly nodded his head then looked up directly into my eyes. I was wondering what was happening when the doctor motioned for me to come to them. I turned to look at Mom and she went with me to see what they wanted.

Mr. Felt said, "The doctor just told me that Megan is awake now and is asking for you, Kylie."

"So I can see her after your visit with her?"

"No, she wants to see you first then I will go in to visit if she feels up to more company. The doctor just said that she really needs to rest so he is limiting her visitors."

"Okay" was all I could get to come out of my mouth. I felt kind of awkward about being the first one to see Megan, but I was also excited at the same time.

Before I left to see Megan, I looked at mom then Mr. Felt took a step closer to me and apologized for staring.

He said, "You look so much like Megan that it is hard not to stare. I have watched you thinking I was seeing her because you even have some of the same mannerisms as Megan and it is just all so surreal. I just wanted to apologize if I have in any way made you uncomfortable."

I stood there for a while before the doctor said, "I will take you to her room."

We walked down the hall a few steps. I stopped and turned to look back at mom and Mr. Felt. I saw them both nod their heads and simultaneously tell me that it was going to be okay. Then, as a tear fell from my eye, I turned to follow the doctor to Megan's room.

We walked down a long hallway. The doctor punched in a code on the keypad next to the large doors. The two huge doors swung open as if following orders. We walked through them and turned right into an intersecting hall. I noticed the sterile smell and noticed the hand sanitizers on the wall next to the doors of each patient's room. We cut through a galley where there were drinks and snacks for the families of the patients. The doctor stopped briefly to say, "If you need something to drink or a snack, this is where you would go to get it."

I thanked him and we moved on, making a right at the opposite end of the galley. Two rooms down the hall, on the right, we stopped in front of room 310. I just stood there for a moment staring at the numbers as I slowly traced them with my finger. I thought of how things might have been if Megan had grown up as Bella. There was this strange feeling even as I stood there that it was as if we had indeed known each other for a very long time. I couldn't get the words that Mr. Felt spoke to me out of my mind. I was deep in thought, so I jumped when the doctor reached out and touched my arm. Then he proceeded to remind me that Megan was very weak and to please limit my visit to thirty minutes. I told him I would keep an eye on the time. I pushed down on the handle of the door, quietly opened it, and stepped inside.

Strangers Yet Sisters

The sound of someone tapping on the door caused me to open my eyes. The door slowly opened and there stood Kylie. At the sight of her, I heaved a sigh of relief and began to weep. She moved toward my bed and asked if I was in pain. I replied, "No, they have given me medicine for that. I am just glad to see you. I have some questions and I believe that you may know the answers."

Kylie just stared into my eyes as if she had questions of her own. I continued talking, telling her that I sensed there was something familiar about her that I couldn't put my finger on.

I said, "We are virtually strangers, yet deep inside of me it feels as if we have known each other for a very long time. This is so strange, scary, and troubling and I don't know quite what to do."

As I was talking, Kylie stood there with tears streaming down her cheeks then she handed me a small item that she had been holding with both hands over her heart. As I took it, I gazed at the picture of the infant and realized it was the same picture that I had picked up off the floor at the hotel restaurant just a couple of days ago. I turned it around, saw the name and date on the back, and read in almost a whisper, "Bella Longhenry."

Kylie spoke with a voice that sounded like sandpaper as she attempted to hold back further tears. "Megan, I believe with all my heart that you are my sister Bella. This is a baby picture of you and it matches the baby picture of you, as Megan Felt, that was found at the Felt cabin. I don't know where all of this is going to go from here, but I do know that we all want to get to know you."

For quite some time now, I had a feeling of not belonging to the people I had known all these years as my Mom and Dad. This was all so confusing to me, but maybe at last I would find out who I really was and just maybe find the answers to all these haunting nightmares that I had been having.

I couldn't help but open up to my newfound sister. I felt as if I needed to catch her up on the events of my life, when I said, "After about seven years of age was when Mom started to become very abusive at times. Before that I was always Mom's "little princess" and Dad's "baby girl". Mom always made excuses for any injury that I had received as a result of her rage so Dad was unaware of the truth. The stitches that I received in my jaw was a result of her hitting me so hard that I fell, knocking a glass bowl off the counter and breaking it. Then I landed on a piece of glass which sliced my jaw open. There was blood everywhere and I thought I was going to die. She panicked when she saw all the blood. She called Dad all frantic, telling him that I had been clumsy and tripped. She just stared at me as she was on the phone, telling Dad her version of the incident. He told her to bring me into his clinic.

"Of course, Dad was the one who stitched me up. He was the one who did all my doctoring. I'm sure that if I would have had to go to anyone else for all my injuries, there would have been some eyebrows raised and serious questions asked. I guess Dad didn't see the ugly side of her that I experienced, so he always believed her. He was always so tender and gentle with me, which was comforting to me. Yet there was a silent understanding between Mom and me and a fear of worse treatment, so I never told a soul about what was really happening. I remember Mom would act so different toward me in public too, and when we were home, I was virtually invisible.

"She was unable to carry a baby to full term. It was after she would miscarry that she would get short-tempered and sometimes violent with me. As a young child, I didn't understand this, but I later learned to stay away from her when she was in this state. After some time, it seemed that she blamed me for her misery, and the good times that I did have with my Mom became less frequent as her bitterness toward me grew. My aunt Kathy would often take me to stay with her during the turmoil. I think that somewhere inside of my aunt, she knew that I was being mistreated.

"When they were certain that mom would be carrying this baby to full term, they told me that I was to be a sister. One day, I overheard mom talking with Aunt Kathy on the phone and that was when I found out that I was adopted. I knew from that day that I would make my plans to leave.

"When I saw you in the hotel restaurant, I thought I recognized you from somewhere. When you introduced yourself, your name sounded familiar, but I still couldn't place where I had met you. I didn't want to get caught and have to return home where I felt like an unwanted pet."

Kylie asked if my scar was the first of Mom's rampages. I turned my head away from her as the painful memory resurfaced. I said, "Yes, that was when she first started being abusive, and it was at that time when I began to believe that I was unwanted. It was so confusing to be treated in that way then have her turn right around and tell me that she loved me. When I left, I swore I would never go back to where I was treated with such disdain. When I discovered that I was adopted, I was able to make the connection as to why it was so easy for her to treat me as she did."

Kylie took this time to talk to me about forgiveness and the importance of it. She said, "Megan, I have seen the effects of unforgiveness and it is not pretty. An unforgiving person gets so swallowed up in bitterness and blame that it consumes their lives. They are very miserable people, and if you know what to look for, you will find unforgiving people everywhere you turn. There was a time in Mom's life when she was unforgiving and we all suffered for it. You see, these people want to get everybody to agree with them and their misery so that they feel justified in all their bad behavior. All the while, God is crying out to them that he is there and will help them to overcome. Some people simply choose to ignore him for their right to be angry. It's not bad to be angry, but it's not good to hold on to it."

What she said made a lot of sense and I didn't want to be unforgiving or angry. It seemed letting go of anger would be a lot easier. This way, I could look to my future with a clearer vision and a lighter load.

Kylie had been in my room for what seemed hours when the nurse came in to remind me that Dad was waiting to see me. Kylie said she would leave, but I asked for a few more minutes with her. The nurse said she would inform my dad then left the room. Not knowing exactly how to respond to my dad, I turned to Kylie for advice. Kylie told me that we should pray and ask God for help and guidance. I was so new to the idea of talking to someone you can't see, so I was glad when Kylie volunteered to pray.

Kylie began, "Father, God, I thank you for keeping my sister alive. I know that things seem very confusing for all of us right now, but I believe that you will work things out. Be with Megan as she talks with her dad and help her to know how to talk with him. I pray for your peace in the name of Jesus. Amen"

When she finished praying, Kylie looked up with a sparkle in her eyes and said, "Hey, do you remember the time we first met at the church gathering?"

"Vaguely, why?"

A grin stretched across Kylie's face. "I just remembered some of the folks there commenting on how we looked so much alike and said that we could be sisters. I just think this is all so amazing that something like that comment could have just as easily been forgotten and now here we are."

I told Kylie, "I remember thinking that I had never seen two total strangers look so much alike as you and I did, but I had no reason at that time to think we were anything other than strangers."

"Well," she said, "I had better go and let Mr. Felt come in to visit. I will keep praying for you out in the lobby. Can I come back tomorrow to visit?"

"Okay." *I can do this,* I told myself. "And you had better come back tomorrow. I would like to visit with all of you at one time tomorrow if the doctor allows it."

"Mom, Dad, and Jeff will be excited to see you. See ya tomorrow."

"Goodbye, Kylie," I whispered.

I took yet another deep breath and exhaled slowly while waiting for the next visitor. I didn't know what to expect and a part of me felt very cold toward Mom and Dad for all the cruel lies that had been my life. It was a feeling of being cheated and used. Then there was this anger that welled up inside of me at the thought of my real parents being put through what must have been even worse pain than what I was feeling. I really didn't know where to begin or how I would even respond to Doc a. k. a. Dad. Right now there was a heavy, suffocating feeling of dread on my chest and I was finding it hard to breathe.

Kylie

As I walked back to the waiting room to talk to the others, I noticed Mr. Felt standing in the hall by himself. I told him thank you and that Megan was ready to see him. With a somber face and a quiet voice, he said, "Okay," and left. I watched him for a while as he walked slowly down the hall. Part of me sensed a great sorrow for him mixed with the question, how could a person knowingly keep all these secrets without extreme guilt?

As I entered the room, I noticed Mom and Adel pacing anxiously on the other side and Pastor and Walt in deep conversation in the far corner of the room. As I scanned the area, Jeff and Dad were nowhere to be seen. Mom noticed my return, broke her pace, and headed straight for me as I continued to look for Dad and Jeff. She informed me that they went for a walk at one thirty and that they would be back at two. I glanced at my watch and saw that it was eight minutes until two, so I took a seat and we waited for them to arrive to talk about my visit with Megan.

"Mom," I said, "I am so thankful that you and Dad are home and safe."

Mom stroked my hair and said, "I am glad that the two of you are home as well."

She looked at me and I saw tears forming in the corners of her eyes. She said, "It certainly has been a journey that I am glad is over. We all have a lot to talk about when we get home. Your Dad and I realize that you and Jeff are so much more grown-up than we have given you credit for."

Megan's Visit with Mr. Felt

The door opened and there stood the man I had known as my dad for nearly fifteen years. He slowly walked into the room with his shoulders slumped and his head down. My thoughts were so loud that it seemed I may have actually spoken the words. *Wow, this is the first time I have ever seen him look so ashamed and without words.*

He moved closer to my bed but seemed almost afraid to get too close. He raised his head slightly, avoiding direct eye contact, but I could hardly see his eyes due to them being swollen. I could tell that he had been crying. I had never before seen him shed a single tear. As he stood before me now, he looked shattered and this moved me in such a way that I broke into tears.

He reached for my hand, still avoiding direct eye contact, and squeezed it gently. Clearing his throat, he began to speak. I hardly recognized his voice as it was very raspy.

He began sobbing. "I am sorry. I am so, so sorry Megan. I don't even know where to start or how to make things right. I can't even imagine what you must be feeling or thinking about me and your mom right now, but we do have a lot of explaining to do. Right now, I really think we all are in agreement that we should wait till you are fully recovered. We just want to focus on that right now."

Part of me wanted to scream out, "I want answers right now!" But then, on the other hand, I was thankful for the extra time to sort things out in my own mind. I didn't say a word. Not because I chose to remain silent. My body just wouldn't cooperate with what was going through my mind, and I decided that it was best to remain silent and just take things in to think on before things were said that I may regret later.

Dad didn't stay very long, but before he left, he told me that he would be back tomorrow afternoon with Mom and Aunt Kathy. Part of me was excited to see my aunt, but I really wasn't overly anxious to see Mom. Right now my emotions were so mixed up that I just wanted to sleep and hope that when I woke, this would all just be a bad dream. I felt so lost, but somewhere inside of that storm was the truth, and I needed to discover my true identity. As the door slowly closed behind Dad, I drifted off to sleep.

Kylie Finds Peace

Once dad and Jeff were back, we all sat down and I told them some of what Megan had shared with me, especially the part where she said she wanted to see all of us tomorrow if the doctor would allow it. I chose not to tell them of Mrs. Felts' treatment of Megan. I figured that she would share that when she was ready.

To ease some of the stress, I shared that part about us two looking so much alike that we could be twins. I looked over at Jeff with a twinkle in my eye. He piped up with, "Then we would have to be triplets."

With that everyone chuckled, which sounded so good to my ears. We talked for forty-five minutes then Mr. Felt came into the room. We made room in our group for him. He told us that he would be going home tonight and would return with his wife and sister-in-law tomorrow afternoon.

Mr. Felt talked with dad about having a meeting tomorrow with a lawyer regarding Megan and the whole mess surrounding her illegal adoption. Dad asked him if all the adults could get together and try to work things out between themselves first. He didn't want any more trauma for Megan after all she had been through. Dad said, "I would like to be able to work this out just between the families if that is all right with you."

Mr. Felt asked if he could think on it and get back with Dad in the morning.

Dad said, "Absolutely," then they exchanged phone numbers as we all were leaving the hospital.

The afternoon and evening came and went with much talk, not only of the past but mostly of what lay ahead for all of us. All of the what-ifs that came to our minds were discussed in great detail, and at the end, it was all handed to the One who knew all the answers to each question. At supper time, we all went to a home-owned, country-cooking restaurant. Walt, Pastor Chuck, and Adel all joined us for one of the most delicious meals I ever recall having at a restaurant. Maybe my senses were just heightened from all the excitement of the past few days, but this meal almost outdid Mrs. Deter's cooking. I could tell by the long wait to be seated that it was a very popular place to eat, even though it seemed to be out in the middle of nowhere. As everyone was enjoying their meal, I couldn't help but notice what the chatter was about at the tables surrounding us.

I overheard someone make the comment, "I couldn't imagine how I would feel in her situation and on top of that being shot."

Another person from the same table chimed in. "Yea, but I sure am glad they caught the outlaws. I feel so much safer with them off the roads."

As they continued in their conversation, I could tell they were talking about Bella. It was the *big* news of the area and seemed to be the chatter wherever we went.

We finished our meal and headed back to the hotel where we all gathered at Pastor Chuck's room to pray and ask God for his direction. Well over an hour had passed as we each petitioned the Father. Everyone prayed at once, and I could feel a presence in the room. This had happened to me before, but I couldn't explain it then. Now I have come to understand that it is the Holy Spirit and he is here in such a strong way because he has been summoned by all the prayers going up at once.

Pastor Chuck had preached about this very thing on several occasions. He talked about God wanting to communicate with us and how he has given us his Spirit, the Holy Spirit, for this very reason. There is even a scripture in Acts that talks about the power of the Holy Spirit coming on people and giving them power from on high. It seems to me to be a very special and intimate relationship with the Heavenly Father. I am still new at this, but I long to have this kind of relationship with God, one where I can sense him in a real way and not be afraid.

When the praying ceased, we all shared what God had spoken to us. Dad started by saying that he prayed for the Felt family, that they would come to know the Lord. There were several "Amens" to that. Dad and Mom both shared how they had thanked God that Bella was still alive and prayed for her salvation as well.

Mom said, "Her salvation is the most important thing now that we know she is alive."

After all the adults shared what they had gotten from praying, they turned to us and asked me and Jeff if we had anything to share. It was a nice feeling to be included in this. Jeff fidgeted, looked down at his untied shoe strings then reached for them and wound them around and around his fingers as he talked about what was on his heart. He told how he asked God to restore our family so that Mom and Dad would be able to stay home.

As I looked around the room, I noticed there wasn't a dry eye after Jeff finished talking. He kept his eyes locked on his shoes the whole time he spoke. His canvas shoes were accumulating darkened circles on them where each teardrop made contact. When he finished talking, he looked up and the tears then streamed down his cheeks. Mom and Dad each put a hand on his shoulder as Dad whispered, "We are in agreement, son."

Mom then turned to me and asked if I had anything to share. I told them that I was thinking along the same lines as Jeff. I had a lot of other questions though, such as: Would Bella be living with us now? Are we moving or do we get to stay in our home? What is going to happen now? All the what-if questions of my young mind. Mom and Dad said they didn't have all the answers but reassured me that my questions would be answered in time.

With all that was on our minds, it was hard to even think of going to sleep, but we all went to our rooms and turned in early for the night. I threw back the blankets and crawled into the bed. There was nothing like sleeping in my own bed at home for which I longed. I just desired to get back to somewhat of a normal life. I say somewhat because the reality is that nothing will be the same because of one event which happened nearly fifteen years ago. Now we all have a lot to adjust to. I had many questions running through my mind, as I often did these days. Where would Megan live? Would she come to live with us? Will she get to be a part of our lives from here on out? Will there be peace between the families involved in this great sadness? And will we all be safe from the ones at the center of all this tragedy?

My mind was reeling from all the questions that made me fear the worst.

Then I started praying and focusing on the Father. I could hear him as if he knelt by my bed and whispered in my ear, "Kylie, I am, and I know the end from the beginning. I am a just God and I will take care of all things in my time. Just trust me."

The Holy Spirit brought a scripture to my mind, so I reached for the Bible on the night stand, turned the lamp on, and looked up Matthew 10:28. It read: "Do not be afraid of those who kill the body but cannot kill the soul. Rather, be afraid of the One who can destroy both soul and body in hell."

I whispered a prayer of thanks and asked God to teach me more of his ways that would keep me walking on the righteous path leading to him.

"With my whole heart, I will put my trust in You, oh Lord, for You truly know all things."

I was finally able to sleep in peace after speaking these words to the One who knows all things and with that truth will I live each day hereafter.